HORROR

Cover art and interior by Joel Amat Güell
@joelamatguell

ISBN: 9781955904940

Troy, NY
CLASH Books
clashbooks.com

HORROR

 @clashbooks @clashbooks  /clashbooks

Email: clashmediabooks@gmail.com

Violent Faculties

Charlene Elsby, Ph.D.

Author's Note:

Submitted in partial fulfillment of the requirements toward application for tenure and promotion within the Department of Philosophy as evidence of research productivity.

Table of Contents

1

The Space in Which Emily Was

The question of how much space a human inhabits can be interpreted multifariously, and I use that word on purpose. How much space does a human seize? That seems like a practical question. How much space does a human occupy? That seems like another one. The focus of the present study is the latter, for the former might be answered by a practical experiment, while the latter might not be.

This is why I've taken Emily.

Emily was generous and sincere. Emily was gorgeous. Emily and I got along so well, until we didn't. The thing is, I think if Emily thought about it, she'd know why I'd done what I'd done.

Emily was fairly quiet, until she absolutely couldn't be.

With a philosophical experiment, we must not only define our terms from the outset, but also recognize that those terms might and should be redefined as the experiment proceeds. This is how knowledge *progresses*. Let's not pretend what we assumed at the outset is how things will turn out. There's no evidence for it. In fact, the opposite is quite certainly the case. The evidence shows that no matter what you've done and plan to do, there's never any plan that works out quite right, is there? Lucretius had to put a swerve into his atomistic conception of the universe in order to explain it, and now *so do we* with Emily.[1]

Let's just assume that things will not turn out as anyone hopes at all.

How much *space* does *a person take up*, i.e., *occupy*, rests on our definitions of "space," what it means to "take up" or "occupy," and of course on what it means to be a "human." For it might be possible to reduce the amount of space a human takes up by taking away their personhood, but to do so would change the experiment—and of this change, we must make note in our discussion.[2]

---

1   In Lucretius' *De Rerum Natura,* tr. William Ellery Leonard. (New York: E. P. Dutton, 1916), he writes of how we're all right fucked for planning anything but that nevertheless chaos is necessary for creation: "We wish thee also well aware of this: The atoms, as their own weight bears them down Plumb through the void, at scarce determined times, In scarce determined places, from their course Decline a little—call it, so to speak, Mere changed trend. For were it not their wont Thuswise to swerve, down would they fall, each one, Like drops of rain, through the unbottomed void; And then collisions ne'er could be nor blows Among the primal elements; and thus Nature would never have created aught."

2   The empirical distinction between "person" and "human" where "human" refers to a species of rational animal and "person" to that person's particularity should not apply. Cf. John Locke, *An Essay Concerning Human Understanding*, Book II, Chapter XXVII, "Of Identity and Diversity" where personhood is something ephemeral and separate from the spatiality of a human. We are here discussing the human and not whatever remains once its limbs are gone: "Cut off a hand, and thereby separate it from that consciousness he had of its heat, cold, and other affections, and it is then no longer a part of that which is himself, any more than the remotest part of matter. Thus, we see the substance whereof personal self consisted at one time may be varied at another, without the change of personal identity; there being no question about the same person, though the limbs which but now were a part of it, be cut off."

Emily, of course, may not weigh in.

Except for initial weigh ins, which are when we determine not how much space, but how much *mass* constitutes the person we know as Emily, who was taken last Thursday from the office where she works. Emily there, day in, day out, sun up, sun down. She's wasted on the menial tasks of the cubicle but *not anymore*; the density of false barriers inversely proportional to the density of her new friends. *Emily, why did you learn to hate me?*

The measurements of space and mass can of course be related by density, and that's where the science departments would love to end things, but that won't do, not here. Still, Emily must first be subject to so many measurements, to set the initial conditions for our experiment. Even so, just by knowing how much space she occupies and of how much mass she is constituted, we still do not know how much space *a human* takes up, not any human, not even Emily. Because by "space," we do not mean merely the amount of void filled by her physical form.

There are many voids a human might fill.

When Plato compared the universe to a child, whose father was the demiurge and whose mother was the space in which the demiurge set to arranging its creation, he made a metaphor that's simply not useful to the present study.[3] For you'll find that similarly to men, women take up space as well. Women are not the empty vessel of creation they have been made out to be. It is obvious to even the most cursory glance that the stuff of which they are made is very similar to the male. It is merely differently

---

3   Plato, *Timaeus*, 50d, tr. Donald J. Zeyl: "For the moment, we need to keep in mind three types of things: that which comes to be, that in which it comes to be, and that after which the thing coming to be is modeled, and which is the source of its coming to be. It is in fact appropriate to compare the receiving thing to a mother, the source to a father, and the nature between them to their offspring."

shaped. Thus, to render the female empty and the male full is an error, for it seems that both are, rather, elements of the sensible world of which Plato speaks—the children of the universe. When you think about it, the metaphor is more confusing than it is enlightening, for if one were to take it at all seriously, it should lead to the question of whether women are, in fact, made of atoms at all, and not void.

And Emily is not void.

Nevertheless, it is an interesting question as to whether Emily and all women might embody the void, as space to be filled, from within a sexual context. And my study will determine to what extent Emily is void and to what extent Emily is atom. But first we must continue setting down some terms.

When we say there is space for a human, we mean several if not many things. Think of a vehicle, for instance, and how many it seats. There is always more room inside the vehicle than there are so-called spaces, and I dare say that many of us have pushed the boundaries of how many humans might fit in a vehicle, if the occasion arises that we need to transport more humans than said vehicle would allow. Two people occupy one seat, and suddenly the space required for a person is halved. What we thought was a limiting factor turned out to be nothing more than a social convention. (But social conventions do not mandate metaphysics; rather, it's the other way around.) We look at places to live and how many rooms there are inside, and we make an estimate of how many people would live comfortably within said space. There might seem, at first, to be a magic number of square feet that would optimize the ration of space appropriate for any one person, but this too is malleable. Depending on your relation to the people nearby, more or less space is required. Love requires less space. Hatred requires more. Except when hatred leads to violence, and then the required space quickly contracts from maximum to none, like the tension between the strong and weak nuclear forces. Far away *and* close.

Emily and I are relatively friendly, or at least we were.

For fuck's sake, Emily, you could have called.

There is a cultural component, where the amount of space a person requires is proportional to how much space a person is used to, such that there are people who require less space just because they have become accustomed to having less space, and so we must conclude that one aspect of how much space a person takes up is habitual, subject to change, rather than natural, inherent.

Emily used to live in a studio apartment downtown. I suppose on the lease she still does, though she is not physically occupying it. Thus the physical definition of occupation and the legal definition diverge.

When I brought Emily in, I designated for her several places in which to exist. Emily was not used to being confined to one room; that much was obvious. But though the space in which she existed had now contracted, there were yet several spaces within the room between which she could move, thus providing her with an array of spaces, so to speak. (The spaces were not physically separate, as it is actually impossible to divide space;[4]

---

4   See Aristotle's *Physics* for a reconstruction of Zeno's argument about Achilles and the impossibility of traversing a finite amount of space: "The second is the so-called Achilles, and it amounts to this, that in a race, the quickest runner can never overtake the slowest, since the pursuer must first reach the point whence the pursued started, so that the slower must always hold a lead. This argument is the same in principle as that which depends on bisection, though it differs from it in that the spaces with which we have successively to deal are not divided into halves. The result of the argument is that the slower is not overtaken; but it proceeds along the same lines as the bisection-argument (for in both a division of the space in a

however, I determined conventional divisions that Emily would recognize owing to our shared habits.) A short form replacement of rooms by creating separate stations within one room. The variety of spaces in which she could place herself became a replacement for the larger spaces in which she used to be free to roam. She was not free to leave the room, but nevertheless, she could roam from one chair to another, to a lounger, to the bed, and thus I inferred that the space in which a person takes up can be effectively reduced by providing a similar experience of *choice*. A person feels they are the inhabitant of a space, not because they physically exist within it, but *because it is within their possible world.*[5]

It's funny, because when the furniture began to disappear, so did the space, at least according to Emily's concept of it. If there was no longer a chair in the corner, she no longer frequented that corner. *Space becomes identified with its contents.* Once I had reduced the room's equipment to two possible placements only, Emily's movements changed as well, moving between those spaces, as if the previously inhabited spaces no longer existed. The spaces in which the old furniture had ceased to exist *died*, became spaces that could no longer be occupied, spaces that once were but now are not. *Despite that, the spaces persisted.*

---

certain way leads to the result that the goal is not reached, though the Achilles goes further in that it affirms that even the runner most famed for his speed must fail in his pursuit of the slowest), so that the solution too must be the same. And the claim that that which holds a lead is never overtaken is false: it is not overtaken while it holds a lead; but it is overtaken nevertheless if it is granted that it traverses the finite distance." Aristotle, *Physics*, 239b14-29, tr. R.P. Hardie and R.P. Gaye, in *The Complete Works of Aristotle*, (Princeton: Princeton University Press, 1984).

5 Cf. Maurice Merleau-Ponty's concept of the body as an *I Can* from the *Phenomenology of Perception.*

When the furniture was removed entirely, all of a sudden, space that was not fit for habitation was fit again, dead spaces came alive. Emily sat on the floor, where she never would have dared sit before, and leant against walls that previously had gone untouched, unnoticed, finite boundaries to her universe.

But we cannot limit our variations to externalities. Certainly the question of how much space a human requires is not determined by objects beyond them. The foundational question of the space in which Emily was relates to her own physicality, not that of others, not that of *things*.

What we mean by someone's physical space is the finite boundary of their flesh, and possibly some of the space around it. This is what we call their "personal space," as if their person takes up more space than their atoms might suggest. What's important now is Emily's space, Emily's own space, a space more intimate than that which surrounds her. The space to invade doesn't belong to her by habit but by materiality itself, and when I told Emily that what I wanted, what I needed from her, was for her to let me into her head, *I fucking meant it*.

Over the weeks, I fatted Emily, and I thinned her, and while she protested both, I do not believe her protestations were in contest to the increase and decrease of her spatiality. Emily seemed less concerned with the resulting malleability of space than she was with my methods, which were not designed for the comfort of the subject. Nevertheless, I noticed that as I fatted her, the space that was once external became internal, and as I thinned her, the space that had been internal became external, while Emily took barely any notice of the shift from externality to internality and vice versa. The physical space of a person is malleable, the boundaries shifting with the material, consciousness expanding with physicality.

I had the sense that Emily believed there were spaces that belonged to her and some that didn't. That contrary to reason, she believed her internal space counted as belonging, while her external space may or may not, or certainly counted as belonging in a different sense. While she possessed nothing, she came to believe either that spaces belonged to her, or that she belonged in her space. (It is impossible to tell through behavioural observation alone.) She began to think of her room as her space, even though she did not own it but inhabit it. In a similar but distinct way, she believed the physical space she took up with her materiality was her space, even when she had grown to fill more of the room and therefore, should have recognized the overlap in space and the shift in the relation of belonging.

At this point it became clear that I had to determine on what basis Emily believed some space to be hers and other space not. To observe the ways in which she formed her opinions on the matter would identify the key factors on which opinions in general were formed, and from any large number of opinions, usually some truth can be discerned. And so, I aimed to begin from general opinions and, from there, to abstract a generally valid law of spatiality for the human being as human—for we know how much space a corpse takes, but the human is so much more than that!

There were times in the study when Emily lost her humanity. But to detail these instances would be very bad for the data.[6]

When I put Emily in the closet and asked her (not explicitly) to adjust, she at first seemed amenable. She moved from side to side, just as she had in the room, and in doing so marked out various spaces in between which to move, which corresponded to differently cognized space. But unlike the room, which was

---

6 And we can't have that.

merely somewhere to exist, the closet became somewhere to strategize. The space was not sufficient, and so Emily took to analyzing the *space*'s externality—the physical barrier marking off the space, in order to determine a way to move beyond it. She even took to *dismantling* the physical boundaries, clawing at the walls, and by doing so increased her allocated space to some small degree, though a futile effort it ultimately proved to be. She took no small amount of joy in reclaiming some amount of space from the drywall, even though with the drywall now on the floor, she had in fact not made any net gain of space but only succeeded in redistributing the space available, so as to be more to her liking. At this point in the study, I concluded it is not about increasing the available space to the subject, but the joy she takes in penetrating something that confines her, of destroying it, of rendering its spatiality undelineated.

We take joy in dismantling the boundary between what is something and what isn't.

Once, before her captivity, when I'd made love to Emily, I said I would destroy her, and now I realized, this is what I'd meant.

In her confinement to the closet, I made Emily as small as possible, to make her more proportional to the physical space she was allowed. But no amount of thinning Emily made her happy to exist in the closet, and I concluded the amount of space she required to surround her physical form was not a mere matter of proportion, but there existed some absolute minimum space in which she conceived it possible to exist, whether accurately or not. So back she came into the room. I allowed her to gain the room, so that I might destroy her again.

I let her get fat, then I cut her back to size, which she took very badly. For although I had granted Emily that additional space, she did not think she owed any of it back to me.

Emily the spacious ungrateful.

Emily who lived in space, existed of it, and dissipated.

Emily for whom there's nothing left but penetration.

The spatiality of a person's body is naturally punctuated by certain access points. And those access points are determined biologically. It seemed natural to experiment with the variable of internality and externality through Emily's mouth. After all, it was an orifice in which things naturally went. But the variety and size of things could differ, and thus the limits of internality as well as externality might be more stringently defined. There was a difference in the internality of something I put in Emily's mouth for her to swallow, and a further difference if the thing she swallowed was meant to be digested. The former was less of an intrusion to her physical space than the latter. Should I put a coin in her mouth, for instance, and ask her to swallow it, she behaved as if the coin were an unwelcome visitor to her physicality who, despite having been invited in, must be removed at once. Emily, who was, after all this time, coming around to believe in my methods and to contribute to our data's interpretation, had observations of her own, which I promised I'd record when there was nothing left. Emily explained, with the coin experiment, she came to know there was some portion of her internal space which didn't belong to her, which the coin had taken, which she desperately wanted back. Increasing the number of coins increased the feeling of intrusion, although that feeling itself was one to which she quickly acclimated. (When Emily was in a thinning phase, other material might find a home within her, with less fuss.)

Emily had other orifices too, and I penetrated all of them. Interestingly, she seemed most receptive to being penetrated with a body part, for at least the material penetrating her body was of a similar sort to that being penetrated. (Is this why humans consume flesh, as an analogue to ourselves?) Thus, she was much more receptive to one, two, three or four fingers in her cunt than she was to any other organic or inorganic matter. I tried the same experiment with her ass but, due to its relative inflexibility compared to her cunt, the experiments were much less adventurous. Emily treated any penetration of the ears or nose as unwelcome. She complained of her airways being blocked if I impeded her nasal cavities, but why she complained of her ears, I surmise a much less immediate sort of reasoning. It seems reasonable that one should worry about the nostrils being impeded, because of the threat to one's life. On the other hand, the threat to one's life due to a blockage in the ears seems remote, perhaps a faraway effect where one fails to sense a proximate danger. Thus, I believe the discomfort produced when Emily's ear canals were impeded was more due to a formed habit of their being free from such impediments, than it was due to fear or anxiety over a loss of life.[7]

Emily's cunt received all sorts of impediments without inducing fear at all. Knowing Emily, it had become obvious she did not think of her cunt as being so much a part of her body as was her mouth or nose, because it was always through her cunt that other people came to access her. And when that happens repeatedly, one comes to confuse the internality and externality of the part, such that the cunt becomes almost an external body part, accessible to all and especially to my instruments.

---

7   I recognize the futility of explaining contemporary reactions according to antiquated survival instincts, as it is no longer the case that one evades death because of the quick response to the passive reception of a sound. I think that if you think long enough, you can imagine an evolutionary argument for just about any observation, and the fact that that is possible, is evidence that it shouldn't be done.

Anything that one uses as a tool, for a purpose or against someone, can be termed an instrument.

In it goes, she'd say during the trials.

Emily as mother, Emily as void, Emily as the vessel of all, is what she became or was all along, the fulfillment of her *telos* as the female variation of man. For her physical form adjusted to all sorts of intrusion through the vaginal cavity, though without these things coming to be conceived of as internal. While they were certainly inside, they were not internal to her space, as were the coins I'd had her swallow. Unwrapping roll after roll of quarters and inserting them, one by one, into her cunt, she at no time became concerned that I should count them again as they were removed, for she was certain that they would not become integrated with her person, and it was because of the orifice through which I inserted them.

As I've said, the mouth was different.

I inserted ever larger objects into Emily's cunt and I took their volume and subtracted it from her physical space, as I had calculated it from her measurements. For now we had a new way of reducing Emily, of rendering her atomistic structure something closer to void. By filling her physical space with other things, the space which properly belonged to *them*, as Emily had believed that the space within the closet had been *hers*. But what if the objects occupying Emily weren't objects?

I brought in men, whose penises ranged from small to large, for as I had above ascertained, Emily seemed most comfortable being penetrated by flesh—and I speculated, flesh without bones—and in this fashion, I would discern whether the human is more conducive to becoming void to objects constituted of flesh, or whether the phenomenon were ephemeral, specific only to my fingering. Perhaps the atoms, to render Emily most void, must be male, as we might infer from Plato. To test all of the flesh, I had the men penetrate her with their arms, and one man, as far as he could make it, with his head. Perhaps earlier in the study, Emily might have resisted, but since I'd let her out of the closet, it was like my laboratory was enough world for her. As the man crouched between her legs, Emily rotated her pelvis upward, a better angle to bury his skull. Even so, he could not submerge past his eyes. Men's hands came from all directions to assist with the positioning and force. Emily screamed, and so did he, forced to reckon with man's worst failing—having grown too large to crawl back in the womb.

I theorized that, if I could fill the empty spaces of Emily with as much flesh as Emily was herself constituted, she would become mere void, by simple subtraction.

And I penetrated her as well. As the men accessed her orifices below, I would put a hand or an elbow into her mouth, for as small as Emily had become, she was yet full of so much sound, and that sound was full of so much agony, as much agony as one might expect from a person who was becoming spaced out of existence. For everything that went into Emily, her space had to retract, take up less, until most of her was not her.

Yet again we reached a limit to how much Emily could become void, and I had to change tactics once again. While Emily had previously protested to cutting, I saw no other way of making the size orifices needed to fit the sorts of objects I deemed necessary for the experiment. So I cut into her arms and made new spaces for the men to fuck, and into her calves as well. I cut into her thighs so that when she lay back, men could approach her from both sides and fuck her in the thighs, the calves, the arms and the mouth at once. I held her down on the floor, my arm inside her cunt, anchoring her against the hardwood. But it still wasn't enough. I cut behind her breasts and let the men fuck her there too. I cut her, until Emily was as much inside as she was outside, as much made of void as she was atom. I cut into Emily until, she told me, she was nothing but a spot inside her head which contained nothing material but only thoughts, mainly thoughts about how the experiment was going, and how it would be written.

The worse that was done to Emily, the less she could recover. While the flesh of a human may stretch and recede, there is a point at which that capacity ends. It's the failure of that capacity that leads to the dissolution of the flesh, the elimination of the conventional boundary between a human and its environment, the point at which a body becomes an object, just another piece of equipment in someone else's space.

I conclude that while discomfort is a measure of how much space a person believes they have dominion over, these boundaries should be considered horizons rather than fixed limitations. Like a horizon, the space in which a human is recedes, the closer one moves to it, until it disappears entirely.

As an appendix to this case, I note a funny thing that happened. For the more things I did to Emily, the better I loved her, but more than that, the worse I was to Emily, the better she loved me too. And when, before she died, she said, "There's nothing else left for me," I told her, "You're the nothing that's left for me, too," which seemed to restore her quiescence at death.

2

The Lips, the Teeth, the Tip of the Tongue

It's the nature of knowledge to advance, and I therefore believe it appropriate that my second experiment serves to emphasize what in the first experiment was taken as a presupposition—that there is such a thing as a unified entity we refer to as human, and that it has some definite characteristics. There was such a thing as Emily, and she was one of a species. Now, the nature of that species is what is here to be defined.[8]

It's an old articulation exercise they teach to aspiring vocalists:

8 At this point, the biologists will scoff and say the question has already been answered, and that it's something to do with the entity's genome; however, if you look closely at the genome of any organism, you'll notice that it's a pattern that has been attributed to some very specific materials constituting not only humans but all animals equally, that while they say it "contains" the information necessary to determine the development of said organism, they in fact don't know what the word means or have any idea of how it's supposed to work, given the emaciated metaphysics to which, as empiricists, they have recourse. Cells with identical DNA develop differently, sure, but what is also true, is that when I refer to a "human" there are very few cases where what I mean by the term is "that genome over there," so perhaps, after 400 some years, it's time to expand the metaphysics in order to be able to explain even the simplest of concepts.

The lips, the teeth, the tip of the tongue, the lips, the teeth, the tip of the tongue. It was "articulation" in the literal sense—how one moves one's physical parts in order to differentiate syllables adequately. We also say that people are "articulate" if they mean what they say and mean it literally, when they use precisely the number of words required to illustrate an assertion.

We always used to say that the human is the rational animal, following Aristotle's definition, where a definition always consists of something's genus and the specific difference (the difference that defines the species). A definition, then, consists of two words, one of which describes the type of something that something is, and the other word differentiating it from all other things of the same type according to some particular characteristic it embodies while all the rest of the other instances of the type do not. In the case of a "human," the animal is the genus and rationality is the differentia. (The human is an animal and what differentiates it from the other animals is its rationality.) But, I told them, when I still worked for the institution, when they—my students—would ask, whether it wasn't speech that differentiated us.[9]

Oh, but aren't they related? I ask them back.

You see, the fact of the matter is, the word we use for "rational" in "rational animal" (λόγος) *is also* translated as "speech"—

---

9 After so many times teaching the same thing to new groups of freshmen, you notice they start to catch on a little more quickly each year, and that sometimes they even begin to anticipate the end of the argument before it's even taught. And you think it's because perhaps the students of this year are interacting with the students of last, but it's in fact much more believable (because they do not, in fact, interact in that way, no matter my tendency to treat them all as one big mass of "student") that the concept becomes habitual within a given human population such that over time, it becomes easier to cognize by successive groups of individuals inhabiting the same space, just like Sheldrake and the mice that proved morphic resonance.

and also account, history, story, logic, sentence, order, etc.[10]— and while we're always focusing on an animal's rationality as a marker of its humanity, in other Aristotelian texts, that which differentiates us from the other irrational, non-speaking animals is that we *speak*.

I must insist, at this point, that this differentiation in no way negates our animality. It is not *not* the case that our rationality or speech or any such differentia renders us non-animal. We are simply the animal that talks and thinks and are absolutely no better, if not worse.

These and other considerations are how we come to differentiate sound from voice. For sounds may serve to indicate or, according to Aristotle, *show something*, like when an animal screams and thereby warns another that danger is nearby. But *voice* "has soul in it";[11] we might say it refers. The human is human not because it cries out "danger," but because it points to the cause of it and gives it a name.

Doctor, please, no, she might say, if she were rational.

Gillian's screams are *animalistic,* we say, precisely because

---

10 See the Liddell-Scott-Jones Greek-English Lexicon for a fuller list of definitions; there are simply too many to provide them here.

11 "Not every sound, as we said, made by an animal is voice (even with the tongue we may merely make a sound which is not voice, or without the tongue as in coughing); what produces the impact must have soul in it and must be accompanied by *fantasia,* for voice is a sound with a meaning, and is not the result of any impact of the breath as in coughing." Aristotle, *De Anima,* 420b29-421a1. Greek text, unless otherwise noted, is from W.D. Ross, *Aristotle. De Anima.* Oxford: Clarendon Press, 1961 (repr. 1967).: (οὐ γὰρ πᾶς ζῴου ψόφος φωνή, καθάπερ εἴπομεν—ἔστι γὰρ καὶ τῇ γλώττῃ ψοφεῖν καὶ ὡς οἱ βήττοντες—ἀλλὰ δεῖ ἔμψυχόν τε εἶναι τὸ τύπτον καὶ μετὰ φαντασίας τινός· σημαντικὸς γὰρ δή τις ψόφος ἐστὶν ἡ φωνή)· καὶ οὐ τοῦ ἀναπνεομένου ἀέρος ὥσπερ ἡ βήξ, ἀλλὰ τούτῳ τύπτει τὸν ἐν τῇ ἀρτηρίᾳ πρὸς αὐτήν.

they are non-representational. They *indicate*, but they do not *represent*. There's nothing specific that they point to. There's no *noun* or *verb* to it. Even the irrational animals can indicate, but they cannot represent. They make sounds, but they have no voice.

They don't have the organs for it.

They don't have the soul for it.

Gillian is no animal, I believe, for the difference between hers and the animal souls is profound.

Maybe she should stop acting like one.

Gillian has, since her capture, been consistently insubordinate. She does not recognize the rationale that guides my actions, not in the way that Emily did, and while I might be tempted to therefore declare her *irrational*, she does in fact disagree *for reasons*, and therefore, I shall not have to replace her with anyone more human, who indeed, may have the same disinclinations.

What Gillian hasn't reasoned is that pain isn't a reason not to go on.

Gillian certainly has voice. Gillian's utterances communicate, express, get something across; the sounds emanating from her do not merely indicate or show just anything, but something specific, something definite, a complex relation or state of affairs with which she voraciously *disagrees*. And they're distinguishable into elements. We try to write the screams of animals as if they were constituted of syllables but, if we're being honest, they aren't. Horses do *not* neigh, and cows do not say "moo." These are projections we've thrust upon them, just for the fact that we've no way to systematize the sounds of animals, and isn't that just my fucking point to begin with? The fact that *the sounds of animals aren't systematic and God damn it Gillian, quit screaming about it.*

A caveat: If we were really Aristotelian, then for this experiment, we'd question my choice of Gillian for a subject, as she's quite female, and Aristotle believed that while women were rational, their rationality wasn't "authoritative." When we relate the alternative definition of λόγος as speech rather than rationality, what the statement means is that nobody listens to women. Long is the history of those who would say that if women are irrational, we can treat them like animals. But fuck those people. We've advanced since then, and it should be obvious to everyone by now that women are rational animals and also capable of speech. We have all the requisite organs for both, and that's what I'm really looking for in a subject—in Gillian.

Not only is the negative argument against Gillian as a research subject invalid, the positive argument *for* her is actually quite convincing. There's a reason why people experiment on the nice animals rather than the vicious ones. And the women here have been trained to be nice above all, so why wouldn't I take advantage of that for my experiment? (While Gillian screams, she exhibits nowhere near the rage of someone more entitled, she is someone who was raised to believe they should be screaming, to think they deserve it.) We experiment on domesticated animals (rabbits, cats, adorable beagles) because they don't bite, even though that makes the experiment sadder, because what have these animals done to us? Nothing. And Gillian? Absolutely nothing. But for my purposes, the fact that she's more docile than the average male subject will work in my favour, and that's precisely why she's here.

I kept Gillian tied to a bed in my office, or rather, now that the nature of my work has shifted focus, my laboratory. My home office. My home laboratory. Which is why I asked her nicely to please be quiet at night, so that in between our sessions, I could carry on life as usual in the rest of the house. It was not ideal, working from home, and without the resources of the institution, but these are my circumstances now, and we all have to work within our confines.

When Gillian arrived, she had a lot to say.

Not anymore, though.

As I said, if you have something to say, you need to have the organs for it.

Gillian is never happy, I've noticed.

It makes sense, because if Aristotle is right, and the essence of the human is to be the rational thing, the speaking thing, and if also according to Aristotle, happiness is defined as something's flourishing, i.e., its having achieved the state of enacting its essence to the fullest extent, then it makes sense that she should be unhappy, as I've denied her the capacity to flourish as a rational animal.[12]

The question is: How do thoughts change, when one is unable to express them? When the sounds become inarticulate. How *do* rationality and speech intertwine, and can a situation be designed such that an alteration in one effects an alteration in the other?

The lips, the teeth, the tip of the tongue.

Another thing I'll note, as it is interesting to me (and therefore, by an inference of shared properties, to the reader as well) that I do not have quite such an empathetic relation to Gillian as I did to Emily. Because I am less familiar with her, because I do not know her, I am not as inclined to pity her situation as I did Emily's. But perhaps it is not familiarity that makes the difference; perhaps

---

12   Aristotle, *Nicomachean Ethics*, 1102a5: "...happiness is an activity of soul in accordance with complete excellence."

it is because Gillian often directs her animus toward me, and in reaction, I conceive of her as less worthy of not suffering. I think there is a phenomenon to be drawn from this observation: we negate the humanity of most of those of whose pain we are the direct cause.

I held Gillian's tongue with a clamp. Ideally, I'd have someone to help with the cautery, but I didn't, and so it had to wait. With the other hand, I cut the tip of her tongue with a scalpel. The way living flesh spreads differs from the already dead in how reactive it is, and how the layers are staggered, each giving up its life as the underlayers remain attached. I thought that of all the flesh she could lose, Gillian should prefer three quarters of an inch of tongue. Nevertheless, as she attempted to pull it back into her throat, the skin, clamped tightly, tore away in bits, and so accomplished my purpose more quickly, although more painfully, and left a more jagged wound than I intended. I continued to sever what was left, top to bottom, far away side to close. She let the blood pool in her mouth and pour over her lips, never thinking to swallow. I had to cut all the way through before I could cauterize. She lost a little more blood this way, which obscured my view and extended the process. But she would make more. There's always more blood.

I noted at this first stage, an observation hardly worth mentioning it is so common: when you can't articulate your words correctly, people doubt your intelligence. We do judge a person's intelligence based on whether we are able to communicate with them effectively. With the tip of her tongue gone, Gillian mispronounced words, was unable to make some sounds entirely (specifically, the dental consonants—d's, l's, n's and t's). But what was also interesting was that in some cases, she developed workarounds—different ways of moving her mouth so she could produce a semblance of the sound at which she was aiming. She *adapted*. And she adapted in the direction of being able to speak without the organs necessary to the task, or at least one of them.

She always wanted to say the same thing.

"Don't," I understood.

It had become more difficult, because of the dental sounds.

The idea was that if Gillian lost the organs she needed to be capable of speech, she would have to lose some of her humanity, as we've come to define it. And the organs were key. By taking away the organs of speech and leaving the organs of rationality intact, I would finally be able to see whether the two were so tied together that to lose the capacity for one meant to lose the capacity for the other.

The lips, the teeth, the tip of the tongue.

Without them, Gillian should become *animalistic*, at least if speech and rationality were as intertwined as they appeared to me. But I had my doubts from the start. That is to say, while I do believe the experiment to be worthwhile, we sometimes hypothesize something we anticipate to be false, in order to prove it so. Sometimes we must test a hypothesis we doubt, in order to prove something isn't the case, when we expect it not to be. What I expected was that Gillian would still be able to express herself, to maintain a complete rationality, even after the loss of her external speech organs—that she would *not* descend into irrationality, into animality, just because she had lost some physical parts.

She didn't have the soul for it.

The medieval authors, too, believed there were ways to render the human animal, but their concepts didn't have to do with deconstructing the physical form. Their moralistic philosophies made it all to do with sin. A man would lose his rationality when overcome by lust.[13] A criminal would lose their humanity through committing atrocious acts, by behaving so *brutishly* we could in effect eject them from the species, declare them animal, and treat them as such, treat them like some woman.

But we can imagine cases where one becomes animal by damaging the organs of humanity—by impeding the rational processes, by damaging the brain. To damage it to the point where one loses their perceptive and rational capacities entirely, with no means of communication whatever—the ancients did wonder if that meant the subject maintained only a vegetable soul, with the capacity to feed and excrete and nothing more.

There are enough of these cruelties already, with their attendant moral circumstances. There are questions of whether we can hold those damaged people morally responsible, and there are questions about what is moral to do to them.

Those are not my questions.

My question is whether Gillian now screams on behalf of humanity or something beyond it.

My question is about the speech-rationality relation and whether removing Gillian's speech organs will give me something that isn't animal at all, but something else, something I anticipated and which, in my view, would be the ideal failure of my experiment. For if I could prove that Gillian wasn't animal, that would remove the theoretical barrier in the way of my declaring her what she was—what I had meant her to be, what she was

---

13   "More over, this lust asserts its power not only over the entire body, nor only externally, but also from within. It convulses all of a man when the emotion in his mind combines and mingles with the carnal drive to produce a pleasure unsurpassed among those of the body. The effect of this is that at the very moment of its climax there is an almost total eclipse of acumen and, as it were, sentinel alertness." Augustine, *The City of God against the Pagans*, XIV, Ch. 16.

meant to be.

Gillian was not an animal.

As I had disfigured her, she was a *monster.*

Aristotle described the monsters too, as those things whose development toward flourishing was impeded. Like when something *should* have two legs but doesn't, because they were taken by war or accident or a madman with a blade. The physical definition of "human"—the two-legged land mammal—no longer applies. But we do not, for that fact, call the human an animal. Rather, it has become monstrous, ugly, unrepresentative of its species.[14]

And so has Gillian.

After the tip of the tongue, I took her teeth. There was virtually no difference between the medical grade pliers and regular needle-nosed ones, if you sterilized them correctly.

Again, I didn't have any help, and I didn't want to cause any damage that I didn't intend to cause. I took a few at a time and let her heal in between in order to make the transition as smooth as possible. The procedure dragged on over weeks, and Gillian got smoother. She became more enclosed. I realized something about myself that must also be true of others—the protrusion of teeth from the face is unnerving, but something we have become used to by exposure. However, as I removed Gillian's teeth and all of what was visible of her became flesh and not skeleton, her physical form achieved a sort of serenity. The face was no longer confused as to which parts were inside and which were outside. The homogeneity of Gillian's visage after I had removed the last of her teeth was, I believe, what made her so beautiful. At each extraction, Gillian would attempt, once more, her plea, as best as

---

14   "The account of the cause of monstrosities is very close and similar in a way to that of the deformed; for monstrosity is actually a kind of deformity" Aristotle, *On the Generation of Animals*, 769b29-30.

she could articulate it: *Don't*.

As the gums healed over the holes left by my pliers, the encasement of her skeleton within her flesh became complete. She no longer had these extrusions that defied the distinction between internal and external. I think that made her not only a more beautiful human, but certainly one more complete. For only now did her inside parts keep their place on the inside.

I brought a male friend to behold her in her new state, to replicate my findings, a male friend whose lust would overtake his reason, as Augustine had anticipated, and would be the one to fuck Gillian—the beautiful monster. I made the intermediate conclusion that Gillian, now with bones all inside and flesh all outside, was in fact less contradictory and more complete. But, of course, this conclusion was well outside the realm of my experiment. If anything, it had something more to do with the relation of internality to externality of my last experiment, which was still probably present in mind. I made a note not to let it skew the results of the current experiment, but I wanted to make sure my intermediate finding wasn't completely subjective—there was something to her new form which made her a more complete being than before.

To obscure the identity of my informal collaborator, let's call my friend "John." John did not share my belief that Gillian was more beautiful than she was before I removed the teeth. But then again, his idea of beauty wasn't consistent with mine. He was likely thinking of her from a social standpoint, wherein he would judge her beauty based on her capacity to bear healthy offspring rather than her capacity to keep her skeleton on the inside. His habitual cognition of the toothless wasn't as something beautiful but as something deformed, and he couldn't appreciate the organism I'd created from Gillian. The lack of teeth has a deep evolutionary connection to illness, which my inspector recognized when he looked at Gillian but did not reflect upon, not enough to see what improvements I had made. Gillian's deformities weren't the result of disease, I assured him. They wouldn't decrease her ability to produce healthy offspring in the least, so he was actually being unreasonable, refusing to admit it—she *was* beautiful. Gillian wasn't traditionally attractive anymore, sure, but maybe the definition was what was off, not my Gillian, not my completion of Gillian, with all of her insides on the inside, where they should be.

I asked him if he would still fuck her, and he said he would.

I asked him if he would still fuck her in the mouth, and he said he would.

I asked him if he would fuck an animal, and he said he would *not*.

I wrote down my finding.

Whatever Gillian was now—now that I'd decreased her capacity to communicate to the point where she could only make the inarticulate sounds of want and fear that we'd expect from an animal—was not in fact animal, on the measure of fuckability.

I asked him to be careful fucking her in the mouth, as some of the wounds were still fresh, and I didn't want to disturb them. In fact, I suggested he clean his cock with the attention of a surgeon preparing to operate, if he wanted to fuck Gillian anywhere at all. John was more than happy to take the appropriate preparations.

Only because I'd been there the whole time was I able to identify the sound that Gillian made, the one which was supposed to imitate, as best she could, her favourite word. But like how we interpret the sounds of animals, I could be projecting syllables onto what are truly inarticulate sounds.

As John fucked Gillian, I noticed, with an extreme displeasure, that her insides were coming out. It turned out I had only contained the solids of her internals. *I had made the same mistake the materialists had made when I failed to consider the fluidity of the human form.* The liquids flowed freely from every orifice, blood and lubricant staining the sheets beneath her pelvis as her tears fell to the side of her face she had turned to me, eyes open but not seeing. The new finding cast doubt upon my previous finding, that I had achieved some higher standard for turning the human form into a container. It's a good thing, after all, that it wasn't the point of my experiment, excited as I was to have been able to conclude it. Gillian bled freely from the reopened wound in her mouth, blood mixing with saliva and vaginal fluid as John went back and forth between her mouth and vagina. Imperfect as they are as inputs (for each input has an output) the commonality between them was blood, and as I noted blood to be the orificial unity, I marveled at how experimentation often yields unexpected results and in this case, unanticipated conclusions. I hadn't accounted for the fluids at all. Thank goodness I had John, to conduct some level of peer review.

Gillian was able to swallow despite her impediments.

One swallow does not make a summer, though.

And I was anxious to get some real findings from my experiment. Did the dead look in her eyes signify progress in her becoming animal?

The lips, the teeth, the tip of the tongue.

Again, I could not keep her clamped, cut, and cauterize the wounds all at the same time. So I clamped, then cut some of the lip, cauterized that bit, then moved along across the orifice. As with so many teeth, it would be too much to remove all of the lip at once, then cauterize. A piecemeal approach was best.

Gillian's sounds now all came from the back of the throat, as if her soul had receded by just that much. Was it enough?

Had it finally made her irrational?

"Now spoken sounds are symbols of affections in the soul, and written marks symbols of spoken sounds," says Aristotle.[15]

If Gillian could no longer speak yet produce written marks, the sort that symbolized affections of the soul, then I could declare the hypothesis false. But the organs of the body meant for writing aren't themselves sufficient to produce it. This is why we take speech to be the ultimate communication, for the system is self-contained. If you have all of your own parts, you can do it. With writing, you require external tools. And yet, if writing is symbolic of spoken sounds, without the spoken sounds, a subject should be unable to write. *That is, assuming the hypothesis is correct*, which I am almost certain it isn't. Writing, I thought, would be sufficient to prove a continuing rationality in my subject. So I handed her these tools and freed her dominant hand.

Gillian took her opportunity and enthusiastically exercised her freedom, her movement, her rationality and her will, to produce the most rational symbol she could. And she wrote on the wall above her bed, in letters as large as she could reach to make them, the single persistent thought she had, which she believed still might persuade me to abandon my experiment and finally leave her be. On the wall, without her lips, her teeth, her tongue, but with her hand, she *said* to me, "Don't."

I still had more to prove.

Some defects brought on by external circumstances, mutations of the genes, are passed down to the next generation and become a permanent part of the genome. In the final stage of my experiment, I would prove that Gillian's deformities wouldn't carry on to her offspring—that her offspring, despite

---

15 Aristotle, *De Interpretatione*, 16a4-5.

her deformities, her monstrosity, would be nonetheless human for it all. It stands to reason that if Gillian had turned animal, she should produce an animal. This, I felt, was the keystone to my experiment. Those moralizing medievalists never thought to question whether the offspring produced by an irrational agent should also become animal, and that if they proved human, that all of their moralizing was false.[16]

I brought John back, day after day, to fuck Gillian in the bed that said don't. Of course, I could have brought him only when it was possible that she would be impregnated. But I thought it better to keep a routine for her, that all the days be the same. For consistency. John assured me that even without the lips, Gillian did not appear inhuman, and certainly not animal. Perhaps he was reassured as I was; the "Don't" on the wall was enough, she *knew enough to object* to what we did to her—she was still in there, a rational animal, and John's growing fondness for her was therefore not of a perverted sort, not the sort of a man for an animal, but the fondness of a man for a woman with whom he has been intimate many times.

When the child finally came, its speaking organs were all where they should be. I declared the experiment complete and disposed of my materials.

---

16 "Democritus said that monstrosities arose because two emissions of seminal fluid fall into the uterus: the earlier one is operative and is not ejected, and the later also enters the uterus, so that the parts of the embryo grow together and get confused with one another. But in birds, he says, since copulation always takes place quickly, both the eggs and their colour cross one another. But if it is the fact, as it manifestly is, that several young are produced from one emission of semen and a single act of intercourse, it is better not to desert the short road to go a long way about, for in such cases it is absolutely necessary that this should occur when the semen is not separated but all enters the female at once." Aristotle, *On the Generation of Animals*, 769b31-770a4.

3

Soul Mates I Kill Shots

Virginia, Faith, and Chastity used to come to the coffee shop where I prepared my lectures on the weekends. They'd sit at the next table, or two tables back, and study together. They went to the Catholic university down the road from mine.

They thought they'd meet their soul mates there.

The weird thing about religious institutions is how opposed to philosophy they are. It wasn't the curriculum itself. It was the same content, but they'd do it differently. In the Catholic universities, when a difficulty arises in the arguments of some philosopher, the Catholic professor tells their students to trust in the Bible or St. Augustine (the man-whore) or St. Thomas Aquinas (the heretic). Even if one part of the course material directly contradicts some other part, the professor will tell those students not to worry about it, because, while there certainly exists a logical impossibility with which to contend, faith isn't limited by the same logical constraints.[17] We, the heretics down the road,

---

17 Cf. John Buridan on how you can't be certain of anything if you believe in God: "Again, the senses can be deluded, as is commonly said, and sensible species can surely be conserved in the organs of

on the other hand, like to pick on the little inconsistencies and figure out the truth of it all behind the matter, *as St. Augustine would actually do*. St. Thomas too. That's why you sometimes hear that philosophy is *hostile* to religion—not because I don't go to work and teach the philosophy of Thomas Aquinas, but because *when I do*, I do it correctly. And that is to say, with the idea that they might learn something.

One of the things those men of God out there (charlatans!) tend to gloss over is the soul.

The religious philosophers, however, do not.

These religious ideas, no matter which religion we're speaking of now, come from Plato and Aristotle, for the most part. "Christians before Christ," the religious philosophers say about these particular Greeks, because they came up with the metaphysics before it had been bastardized. And the apparent contradictions between those religious philosophers (and their respective religions) always come down to which Greek the religious philosopher is faithful to. Is it the man with the tri-partite

---

sense with the sensible things absent, as it says in the *De somno et vigilia*. And then we judge about what does not exist as if it existed; hence we err through the senses. And the difficulty is greatly augmented in that we believe from the Faith that God can form the species of sensible things in our senses without the sensible things being present, and He can conserve them for a long time; and then we judge as if the sensible things were present. Further, since God can do this and even greater things, and you do not know whether He wishes to do this, you do not have certitude and evidence whether you are awake and there are men before you, or whether you are asleep. For in your sleep, God could produce sensible species as clear as, or rather, a hundred times clearer than could be produced by sensible objects. And you would then judge formally that there are sensible things before you, just as you now judge. Hence, since you know nothing about the will of God, you cannot be certain of anything." Joannes Buridanus, *In Metaphysicien Aristotelis Quaestiones,* Paris, 1588. Reprinted by Minerva B.M.B.H., Frankfurt am Main, 1964.

soul, or is it the one whose God is the form of forms?

If you asked Virginia, Faith or Chastity what the soul was, they'd have something to say about it, something parroted from a priest or a minister or a god damned fucking flyer. It's your core, they'd say; or it's what you really are; or it's the part that lives on after you die. But they can't answer any questions for which they haven't been given the script.

How your soul *mates* with someone else's—that's a hell of a question.

Some cunt of a philosopher who no longer gives a fuck might point out that any good God doesn't abide a logical contradiction, so you'd better figure it the fuck out.

The idea of soul being immortal isn't a problem at all, if soul is a motive force, form, for the sake of which all is done, or some other general term, but the problem with the religious philosophers is they all want their souls to be very *particular*—not just a soul but *my soul*. They want the person to live on, as they are, with all of its memories, probably. They want to find their soul mate to live with and die *with*, then live *with* after death, just like death didn't happen, like the soul in the body will be the same after death as it was in the body, like they'll even *look* the same after death. Basically, just carry on. But the soul can't be a physical thing, on their own account, because the defining characteristic of the physical is its propensity to perish, and can you imagine if souls never dissipated? All those souls encased underground in their boxes? So what the fuck?

What the fuck, indeed.

Plato had a theory about people whose souls resembled their physical forms after death. He said that in life, they had become too attached to physical things, and so their soul began to resemble a physical thing. You'd see them wandering through the graveyards at night, trapped.[18] Now it's a common trope. Ghosts stick around, because of some failure in life. *Something that needs correction.*

But Chastity, Faith, and Virginia, they were good girls and not attached to the physical at all. They'd drink decaffeinated beverages and talk about the boys in their classes, as if they were hoping to get a proposal before the end of term, so they wouldn't have to write finals. They'd say there wasn't anything that could make them have sex before marriage, that their soul mates would understand. Their soul mates would have to understand that their first priority was a God-man who made all their souls good. They'd sit there and talk, as if it were a competition, who could be more faithful to God but also to man, who could speak without thinking, hear without ears, and act without reasons. A soul can be good or bad, but also it doesn't change, except depending on what you do, and it's your fault if your soul is bad, but Jesus made them all good, except for some of them, who didn't like Jesus and who deserved whatever they got, not that they would think such horrid things, except of the people who deserved it, so they'd say, and they'd carry on like that every weekend.

They were perfect.

When people around that age get together, you notice after a while they start to meld a little bit. They form an organism, so that each fulfills a vital role. (Though sometimes, one does overtake and destroy the others.) I pictured Faith, Chastity and Virginia

18   Plato, *Phaedo*, 81c-d: "We must believe, my friend, that this bodily element is heavy, ponderous, earthy and visible. Through it, such a soul has become heavy and is dragged back to the visible region in fear of the unseen and of Hades. It wanders, as we are told, around graves and monuments, where shadowy phantoms, images that such souls produce, have been seen, souls that have not been freed and purified but share in the visible, and are therefore seen."

as Plato's three classes of the ideal city—the philosophers, the guardians, and the craftsmen. And of course Plato's ideal city is actually the "soul writ large," because it represented his vision of the soul as composed of three parts—the rational, the spirited, and the appetitive.[19] Just by saying that much, he's moved beyond the capacity of the average Christian to conceive of what the soul might actually be. *And for fuck's sake, it is not a sin to describe it.* While the soul must be everywhere in the body, it can be generally localized, so that the appetitive part remains with the organs of appetite (lower abdomen), the spirited part that makes your heart race when you're angry or in love, and the rational part in the head—the highest part of the physical human form, at least in a standing position—an "upright" stance. Faith, Chastity, Virginia, they were all the same person with small variations. But the variations, I think, weren't big enough to ruin the experiment I'd imagined. They were all *relevantly* similar. Everything about them that mattered was exactly the same. The only way to tell them apart was through little incidental things that wouldn't matter much—not in life, and not in the laboratory.

Virginia said to her friends one day at that café that she had a soul mate, and she said she loved him. I have a difficult time believing people when they say they love something or someone. People are insincere. And if Virginia really believed what she said she believed, she'd know about the fallibility of man, that finitude is a sin, and that love is a passion—and a passion is something

---

19   Plato, *Republic*, 580d-e: "The first, we say, is the part with which a person learns, and the second the part with which he gets angry. As for the third, we had no one special name for it, since it's multiform, so we named it after the biggest and strongest thing in it. Hence we called it the appetitive part, because of the intensity of its appetites for food, drink, sex, and all the things associated with them, but we also called it the money-loving part, because such appetites are most easily satisfied by means of money."

to suffer.[20]

His name is Mark, like the gospel or a target.

The idea of a soul mate, though. It seems to depend on the idea that the soul is in some way incomplete, which brings up a lot of questions. Is not your soul a little bit defective, until you're married off and can finally fail out of college? Does that defect not prevent you from achieving immortality, as long as it's still a thing? Is your soul actually only a *partial* soul, until it's completed by some other *partial* soul? (And what if we're assuming the parts aren't complementary?) But if two things are to "mate," there must be two of them, n'est-çe pas? *For in all relations, there must exist two relata; otherwise, the relation is mere identity.* Does a bit of your soul die when your partner does? They might go for that last one. But they'd explain it away with a metaphor that reduces it to the fact that they're just sad.

Sad.

Sad and perfect.

How does one *mate* with a soul, really?

Let's find out.

Semen is interesting, because it's a way for the male of the species to externalize the soul. Little bits of soul shoot out and are either received or not, and if they are, they can find completion in another bit of soul in order to make yet another one. When the ancients discussed how the soul was transmitted from parents to children, they got very technical about it.[21] The explanations

---

20 The word "πάθημα" in Liddell-Scott-Jones translates to that which befalls one, suffering, misfortune, "passion" in the sense of the passion of Christ (τὰ παθήματα τοῦ χριστοῦ from Corinthians), emotion, condition, affection, incident, feeling, also trouble or symptom.

21 Aristotle, *On the Generation of Animals*, 716a5-18: "For, as we said above, the male and female principles may be put down first and foremost as origins of generation, the former as containing the efficient cause of generation, the latter the material of it. The most

now are all mechanical, leaving no room for the soul at all. But perhaps the fact that children come from the irrational part of a woman's body explains why those children are completely irrational, even far beyond the point in their lives when they can stand on their own. (Plato said the head is round because it's the most divine part of the human and the part physically closest to God—while standing, that is. The head is only the highest part of the human physical form if it's not lying around all day, demanding to be carried.) When the girls discussed their soul mates, they acted as if it would be a meeting of *minds*, by which I think they meant the rational parts of souls. They would find someone who loved them for *who they really are*, and through God's magic, they would carry out God's plan of making babies with their soul mates. But when two people love each other very much, and they want to express that love, they don't just bang their heads together and wait for a baby to exist.

Bits of soul, rather, are exchanged through fucking.

Does it matter where?

It's clear why Faith's parents named her "Faith." I imagined Chastity's parents named her for a misdirected optimism and probably some social concern about having the most Christian name for a baby one could find. I assumed Virginia's parents

---

convincing proof of this is drawn from considering how and whence comes the semen; for it is out of this that those creatures are formed which are produced in the ordinary course of nature; but we must observe carefully the way in which this semen actually comes into being from the male and female. For it is just because the semen is secreted from the two sexes, the secretion taking place *in* them and *from* them, that they are first principles of generation. For by a male animal we mean that which generates in another, and by a female that which generates in itself; that is why in the macrocosm also, men think of the earth as female and a mother, but address heaven and the sun and other like entities as progenitors and fathers." See also footnote above on Plato's *Timaeus*.

were stupid, and they wanted a name that sounded like "virginity" and didn't know about the name "Chastity." Of course, there's no way to know, and perhaps it was all coincidental.

One day at the café, I told Faith, Chastity, and Virginia I'd help them with their philosophy homework, if only they'd come over, to my home, where I kept my texts. They weren't afraid of me. Nobody is. People make a lot of assumptions about me they shouldn't. It's the price I pay for not being taken seriously in general—not in work, not in life, and now, *not as a threat.* There was no other way to do it than to have them come over. Trying to take three at once would be destined to fail. So we made a plan, waited the appropriate interval between, during which time I took the opportunity to tidy my notes, and when the day and time arrived, my subjects came to me.

Now the issue, to be clear, wasn't corralling my subjects. It's easy not to cause suspicion. Just act like nothing's wrong.

Fear is in the heart as well.

No, the issue was certainly the fact that through a carefully curated set of premises that constituted their upbringing, Faith, Chastity and Virginia had become so unbearably boring I couldn't stand to be around them for any longer than was absolutely necessary. There was nothing, absolutely nothing, they could contribute to the data besides their souls.

The three of them went down with no significant issues.

I asked Virginia to help me get some beverages together, and she went down in the kitchen. I asked Chastity to help me get Virginia into bed, so she could sleep off whatever was bothering her, and Chastity went down too. I called out to Faith that something was wrong with Chastity, and Faith went down third. They all woke up in the laboratory.

I couldn't have them making sounds.[22]

Since the purpose of the experiment didn't have anything to do with their vocalizations, I determined the most efficient way to quiet them would be to damage the vocal cords. Go for the source. It was an area where I was not an expert. Trepanning, I had studied. Trepanning was still commonly requested of professionals willing to engage in the practice, for there continues to be a strong faith in its spiritual effects, a homeopathic remedy for suffering, conducted at home with a drill. Traching I'd only encountered incidentally; its spiritual effects being also incidental, related to mutism, which one might also accomplish by simply not speaking. (But there's no way to will a hole in the head.) I worried to some extent that by doing anything to their throats, I might cut off their air supply or hit an artery in their necks that could vanquish them. But if I trached them, I thought I would be able to silence them without getting near anything essential. So that's what I did. It's amazing what one can accomplish if one is resourceful and has resources. I couldn't concern myself with how the little surgeries might be irreversible, or how sterile the conditions were in the laboratory. The experiment would be over long before any of that mattered.

By the time they woke up, it had already begun.

The reason that the ancients thought the soul was in the heart, is because you can feel it change when psychic changes happen. When you love, when you're afraid, when you're angry— the soul has an effect on the physical heart and its rhythms. And that makes sense for the heart, but why the rational soul is in the head is less clear. There's no *obvious* physical change in the head, when one's rationality is affected, except perhaps a

22 See previous experimental results against the hypothesis that their silence bespoke irrationality. It's important to the present experiment their rationality remain intact, at least where Faith is concerned.

headache after drinking. But an even more relevant idea than the body and soul altering one another, and in very definite spatial locations, is the *kill shot*.

Kill shots are the ultimate affect. Affecting the human physical form destructively in any of these places kills the human instantly (while other shots do not), which is to say, a kill shot is a wound inflicted upon a human in such a place that the human will die. The soul is not at all in the hand, because we can live without that. Neither is the soul in the knees, for it's possible to survive an injury to those parts. The highest part of the soul must be in the head, because to penetrate the head with a bullet results in instant death. The spirited soul must be in the heart, because to create a sucking chest wound creates immediate cessation of life. And the least important part of the soul must be in the abdomen, but more dispersed, and that's because it's a *slow* kill shot. Aim for the arms and legs, and the human will still try to flee, but if you want to destroy the soul, you've got to get them instantly.

Kill shots aim for the soul.

Can a soul mate's soul bits transmitted through the semen replace what is lost through a kill shot?

The question is: if I inflict a kill shot on these women, a wound that *should not heal*, can that wound be in any way mitigated by artificial insemination? The replacement of lost souls through the injection of semen into the wounds from which those souls seep? If I were to *almost* kill these women, could the life-creating ooze emitted by their many soul mates replace what soul is lost? If death is the loss of the soul, and if the soul is transmitted through the semen to the woman who acts as its vessel, who provides the material for the production of a new life, who mediates the human form from its origin in the scrotum to the offspring produced, then it only stands to reason that if I put a hole in something that should kill it, continuous fucking should keep it alive.

Are cum shots the cure for kill shots?

I began advertising the experimental set up weeks ago. Of course, I couldn't have the men poking all around in my girls the entire time from arousal to completion, so I carefully instructed them to prepare themselves according to my exact specifications in advance of their interaction with the research set up. I prepared the laboratory like a dungeon with three glory holes. The men would have to arouse themselves manually until such a time as their contribution was necessary to the experiment, and then they'd release their soul-saving ejaculate into one of the three holes, as determined beforehand through a numbering system I'd assigned in advance.

The first hole is Virginia. I used her navel as a guide for where to put the hole, and I made sure it was deep and wide enough so the cock wouldn't have to stretch it. There was a measured amount of damage I wanted to inflict, and I didn't want the men doing more. The second hole is Chastity. I tried to be more careful, because the hole is in her chest. The third hole is Faith, and I had to be extremely careful with her. *It is important for the experiment that these girls are not already dead when the fucking commences.* If the soul in semen is to act as medicine for the kill shots I inflict, there must be some period of time during which the circulatory system is still active, so that the injections of soul may work their way around the body. What's dead is dead; we are not attempting a resurrection (not yet). But will adding soul to something that has lost it increase its longevity?

To give Faith any chance of surviving the trepanning, I had to make sure that bits of skull weren't projected inward. The men would certainly cause more damage to her, because I hadn't prepared the hole as well as I had for Virginia, but if there were enough soul in the semen to cover the damage I'd inflicted, she should survive measurably longer than anyone else might with her wounds. The ideal result of my experiment is that Faith would remain alive after all the men had come, her rational soul replaced with the appetitive soul spewed from so many cocks. In my wildest dreams, I'd ask her what she thought of, her rationality replaced with whatever makes a dick work, and she'd be able to speak it to me, before ultimately expiring.

I put the hole in the side of her head, so as not to ruin her pretty face.

In the room, I'd built a plywood divider that stretched its length. Another material would have softened the blows, but it would have cost more, and my research as of late has been subject to budget constraints. On the boards, I installed handles, to which I attached my lashing straps. Those lashing straps would tighten with the ratchets to a degree so customizable, I could account for all sorts of motions. When I purchased this lab equipment from the home store, the cashier had asked me if I were moving. "Moving!" I laughed, picturing my girls trying to move under the force meant to secure heavy loads on long highways, "Not if I have anything to do with it."

He laughed.

I laughed.

"Actually," I thought, remembering one last thing. "Do you also sell peepholes?"

"Are you planning to do a lot of peeping in the new place?"

"Why, yes," I said.

He laughed.

I laughed.

I paid cash.

Faith, Chastity and Virginia, I made them all face me, so that I could see how long it took them to die. Though to be honest, they all looked a little dead already. They couldn't scream, and it seemed as though they didn't want to cry. Or maybe I couldn't see the soul in their eyes anymore, because it was trying to hide. But it couldn't hide from me; it had nowhere left to go. Nowhere to be. Or more accurately, nowhere to come back to. If the soul could run away from a kill shot, it wouldn't be a kill shot.

I sat down in my office chair with my note pad; it was almost time. I had vetted the men as they were selected. Each had to attest that the semen they offered was healthy and rife with soul; they had to provide assurances that they could ejaculate at their allotted time, and there could absolutely not be any issues with punctuality. A break in the line would ruin my specimens. I gave them a key code for the door and an estimated time of arrival and told them they'd each have two minutes to ejaculate. If a man became greedy, there was very little I could do about it. Thank goodness people do as they're told. I set the peephole in the plywood divider, angled such as to see the mirrors I had hung in the corner of the room. Of course, I had considered cameras. Of course, I had. But I couldn't risk videos being intercepted. My observations are accessible through live stream only.

My research is proprietary.

I think the men liked the set up, because they could pretend that on the other side of this wall, there weren't any humans.

I could see how hard the first cock was already. He either got aroused on the way over, or prepared himself deliberately, so that I'd think his cock was always that hard. But I only ever cared about how hard a man's cock was because he cared. We always have to adapt to their frameworks of what's considered important or not. Faces are unimportant; my evaluation of his masculinity as measured by rigidity, very important. It's the patriarchal contagion—you learn to think like them, to care about things that don't matter, to hate things that don't deserve it. Honestly, sticking out of the fly of his grey athletic pants in the mirror, it resembled the wiggly little animal the medievals used to claim was separate from the man as a whole. An animal that flopped like a rabbit's ears and wiggled like its nose, seeking something in the haphazard way an amoeba attempts to find nutriment, by trial and error, until by chance it locates something to absorb and as such, is allowed to live.

Less than a minute after entering the room, he stepped over to Faith, and I was happy to see that he would not deviate from his assigned duties through some delusion of free will. Faith needed the most soul to stay alive, because of where her hole was, in the skull. For every cum shot Virginia would take today, Chastity would take two, and Faith would take three. The reasoning is, the faster someone might die from a wound to their area, the more semen (soul) they would need to stay alive. So the rotation went Faith-Chastity-Faith-Chastity-Faith-Virginia, Faith-Chastity-Faith-Chastity-Faith, Virginia. And so on, until we ran out of semen.

I surmised they'd think the blood was from a period. (Men only pretend to think it's gross so they have something to hold against us.)

In the mirror, I saw the short, portly man stop thrusting. A squeal was audible through the boards, and the creak of the plywood against the brackets ceased. His head moved back as his neck went rigid, as if the semen were flowing from his entire body instead of just the cock. Faith's eyes got wider as she took her first cum shot. I'd assume it was some kind of fear, but it could also be the soul of her head swelling, as it should.

The second cock was smaller, but no less enthusiastic.

Chastity took her cum shot.

I saw a condom on the third cock, and I had to interrupt the experiment for a moment and enter the waiting room to remove it, and to make it clear such things were contraband in this context. Evidently, he thought he was clever, but if he were allowed to keep it, my results wouldn't be reliable. There was no point in this if there wasn't a cum shot.

As I retreated behind the partition and the experiment continued, I noticed that Faith's reaction to the third penetration wasn't the spontaneous motion arising of itself such as a soul entering the body might cause. For there are motions in which the body might engage despite being restrained—movements of the eyes, of the mouth, of the fingers and toes. Some tiny bit of motion to convince it of its freedom. When a body is restrained, it discovers all sorts of ways to move, and up until this point, those movements would have been some comfort to her, enough to convince her that she was still alive and might continue to be. When those peripheral motions ceased entirely, that's when I knew she was gone. All that's left is the material now. I've heard the men say before, "a warm hole is a warm hole," so I knew they wouldn't mind carrying on with the experiment, and besides, it would take her a while to cool. The blood flowed, but not copiously, as without the functioning brain to support it, the heart no longer bothered pushing it upwards.

Chastity's life wouldn't sustain long, either. If her soul mate existed, it wasn't either of the first two men to bestow upon her their cum shots. The vigorous fucking increased the severity of the wound I had started for her; blood, everywhere, running down the front of her body, separating into two streams where her legs spread, each foot strapped separately to the boards, division by cunt, blood dripping from her toes, soaking both sides of the plywood, blood pooling on the floor, semen beside, within, all around. I'd hoped some of the semen would get caught in the bloodstream and circulate a while; transmutation of the soul, another chance at life. How long did she live, at the end, with someone else's soul in her?

With so many men left to go, I thought I might set down my pen, keep track in my thoughts how much semen Virginia had absorbed into her abdomen, and let them fuck away until they tired themselves out.

About my observations, I should make clear that the thing about medical science is that it's less certain than the other sciences. When we talk about causality in medical science, it's never a certainty and always a probability. I knew, coming into this, the results would not be reported as generalizable principles, but case studies are published in this way, too, such that future scientists might gather the data and recognize the patterns between them. The fact of the matter is, not everything is generalizable. Some things only happen once.

The thing about time is that it's finite, and while Virginia was still hanging on for her soul mate, Chastity and Faith failed to meet theirs in time.

I don't know whether they died faster or slower than they would have had their wounds been left unfucked, semenless. (I would need a control group to properly test my hypothesis, and a new set up informed by the observations made here, today.) I only know how fast they died.

I turned around from my desk to call time on Virginia, and a man's eye was up against an errant hole in the boards.

So I poked him in it.

The relevant conclusion to be made, I believe, is only that there may be some merit to the concept of soul mates, and that today, none of my subjects met theirs. No matter how much soul was fucked into my subjects, none of it continued their animation. I believe it was John Duns Scotus[23] who supported the particularity of forms, and there may be something to it. It wasn't just *soul* they needed, but some *particular* soul still out there.

---

23 It was. I'm just using "I believe" as a false modesty or possibly a rhetorical device.

Interim discussion: A note on the theoretical grounds for conducting philosophical experiments and ethics in research involving human subjects

Kill them, because they're humans.

In the philosophy department, we weren't expected to complete the mandatory training in human research ethics the other faculty members had to, because our research didn't involve humans. But they're working with a very limited definition of "involve." They're generally relying on a concept of "involve" that reduces to whether or not the research has the capacity to harm any particular humans in the immediate future, whereas philosophy only has the capacity to harm all of humanity, for all time.

We come up with the ethics for the other departments to follow. *How to treat humans* is one of our specialties. The focus of our research is existence, truth, beauty, knowledge, and the good. But, for some reason, my colleagues who research ethics don't use humans in their research. For some reason or another, we don't use humans *in our research of the theories regarding what is right and wrong to do to them*? I don't research ethics in any way that's recognized by the academy, as I've seen the inside, and from here, the study of ethics doesn't seem to have anything to do with what humans do to each other.

There's always a good reason to do whatever you want to someone else.

And yet to recognize these failures is not to solve them. Unfortunately, with regard to the ethical treatment of humans, whatever that means, I still don't have an experiment to demonstrate the right and wrong ways to go about things. I don't have a set up to test whether X is right to do to humans and Y is wrong to do to humans, or indeed, humanity.

Even if I came up with one, and figured it all out for them, I don't think they'd listen.

Instead, we merely agree it's wrong to want to hurt humans. Another tide of reasons comes rushing in. Reasons as to why the people I want to hurt aren't humans at all. Reasons why they shouldn't be counted among the people who can't be hurt. Reasons why these people in particular should be *dehumanized*. Dehumanization is a form of harm as well, and you can only do it to people by definition—by creating a definition of "human" that excludes some of them—so it's all together wrong. Not just ethically or morally, but also in the sense of being false, untrue, or inaccurate. We (the humans) dehumanize other humans all the time, in order to do what we want to them—we hurt them once, in order to hurt them again. We take away their humanity, by definition, so it's all right to do all the things you *just can't do* to humans.

But.

I don't believe you have to prove someone isn't human before you hurt them.

Take the whole field of abortion ethics, for example. On one side, there are people trying to prove that a fetus is a human, and therefore it's wrong to extinguish it. On the other side, there are people trying to prove a fetus isn't a human, and therefore it *isn't* wrong. A fellow graduate student explained the whole thing to me outside of class one day, because I couldn't understand why *that's* what the arguments came down to. She explained to me the basis of the arguments on either side, the ins and the outs of whether something is a human and whether that means some other human is responsible for it, and when she was done, I asked her, "Why not just admit it's human, and kill it anyway?"

She didn't say anything.

She should have said, "Because it's wrong to hurt humans." That's what she was thinking, but she didn't say it. She just assumed I would think it. *All humans would.* Except I didn't.

We don't.

The reason everyone has to argue about what's wrong to do to humans, is because we *do* want to hurt them.

We *don't* think it's wrong to hurt humans.

They've got it coming.

What the abortion ethicists are ignoring is that every fetus worth the argument is a *human fetus*, a mere fetus, for sure, but a fetus *of a kind*, a sort, a genus. It's a fetus primarily, and when someone asks, "What kind of fetus is it?" someone else answers, "Human." "Human" is a modifier and not a substance, in this case. When we admit *both* terms exist, the debate is stifled, because no longer are we arguing whether it's all right to kill a human or to kill a fetus but the whole term together—the *human fetus*. But it is all right to kill a modifier.

It's fine.

When "human" is the modifier, on the other hand, all ethics are off. No one's going to condemn you to eternal hellfire for killing a human mannequin, a human image, a human *anything*, as long as there is an *anything* to follow whatever it is that's *human*. It's only when it's a human *simpliciter* that, all of a sudden, we have a problem. And that's all if we're going to humour ourselves with technical arguments. Really, what we need to admit is that if this thing weren't a *human* fetus, it wouldn't be up for abortion. If it weren't at least *a potential human*—if it weren't threatening to, at some future time, turn into a human—then no one would be trying to abort it in the first place. (Note: something that's a potential anything *is not that thing*, by definition. Nothing is potentially what it already is, and so a human fetus, being potentially a human, is therefore not a human.)[24]

More to the point, humanity *is* the threat that makes me wish death upon the fetus. If it were going to be anything other than a human, I could find a way to deal with it, because our standards for how we treat everything but humans are so much lower. But the last thing I want to happen is more humans coming into existence—more things with moral immunity, more things we have to rationalize away if we want to do them any harm whatever. More things with moral impunity, with the capacity to ignore every conclusion of every ethical study, who just go about inflicting their harms at will, in such a way that only the human threat can.[25]

The point is, if they weren't at least *potential* humans, we wouldn't need to abort them.

---

24   Aristotle, *Metaphysics*, 1049a10-18: "And in the cases in which the source of the becoming is in the very thing which suffers change, all those things are said to be potentially something else, which will be it of themselves if nothing external hinders them. E.g. the seed is not yet potentially a man; for it must further undergo a change in a foreign medium. But when through its own motive principle it has already got such and such attributes, in this state it is already potentially a man; while in the former state it needs another principle, just as earth is not yet potentially a statue, for it must change in order to become bronze."

25   Perhaps if we stopped hurting us, we'd stop hurting us in return.

And in much the same way, if none of these people were humans, I wouldn't want to kill them.

Most everything we want to hurt is human. Most everything else isn't worth it. So we dehumanize the humans, whose moral immunity is meant to protect them from harm, in order to make it all right again to harm them. You can blame that one on Boethius, who said that when humans sin, their souls are damaged to the point that they lose their human soul and maintain only an animal one.[26] *Then we can treat them as animals*, has always been the idea. *But it wasn't our fault; they dehumanized themselves*, religious philosophy says. Throughout the history of humanity, some part of it has always aimed to dehumanize some other part and by doing so, the aim is the same. To skate around the moral imperative that it's not all right to hurt humans by taking someone's humanity away from them.

But again, it's something you can *only* do to humans.

You can't dehumanize something that isn't human.

Why all these rational gymnastics?

No one is willing to defend the claim that it's all right to hurt

---

26 Boethius, *The Consolation of Philosophy*, Book IV: "One man, a savage thief, pants after and is ravenous for the goods of other people—you can say that he is like a wolf. Another man, vicious, never resting, has his tongue always in motion in lawsuits—you can compare him to a dog. One man, the hidden plotter, lying in wait, is glad to steal by his deceptions—he can be said to be the same as the foxes. Another roars, giving free rein to his anger—he may be believed to have within him the spirit of the lion. One man, a coward, is quick to turn tail, afraid of things that he need not fear—he is thought to be like the deer. Another, indolent and slack-jaws, is simply inert—he lives the life of an ass. One man, fickle and flighty, changes his interests constantly—he is not at all different from birds. Another wallows in fowl and unclean lusts—he is held under by the physical delights of a filthy sow. And so it is that anyone who has ceased to be a human being by deserting righteousness, since he has not the power to cross over into the divine condition, is turned into a beast."

humans.

No *human*, anyway.

I can't fathom what my experiments might amount to, if my subjects were actually dehumanized—if it turned out my subjects weren't humans at all, but something else, something it's more all right to kill. If my subjects weren't human, all of my observations would be invalid. At no point in my experiment can my subjects be anything other than human, for the mere fact that it would invalidate the whole experimental endeavor.

It doesn't take an experiment to show that you can't take someone's humanity away from them. It's a bad faith concept all around. That's the sickening part of it. People only do it to other people. Doing it to other people is what makes it fun.

The only real dehumanization is death.

You can see it, after death—that nobody is really a materialist. Nobody really believes the human body is what makes somebody human. No one really believes a human corpse is a human. They don't believe the living and the dead are the same. In death, it's obvious to everyone that the body is not a human, the corpse is not a human.[27] A corpse doesn't think and reason. It doesn't see

---

27 Aristotle, *Metaphysics*, 1044b29-1045a6: "There is difficulty in the question how the matter of each thing is related to its contrary states. E.g. if the body is potentially healthy, and disease is contrary to health, is it potentially both? And is water potentially wine and vinegar? We answer that it is the matter of one in virtue of its positive state and its form, and of the other in virtue of the privation of its positive state and the corruption of it contrary to its nature. It is also hard to say why wine is not said to be the matter of vinegar nor potentially vinegar (though vinegar is produced from it), and why the living man is not said to be potentially dead. In fact they are not, but the corruptions in question are accidental, and it is the matter of the animal that is itself in virtue of its corruption the potency and matter of a corpse, and it is water that is the matter of vinegar. For the one comes from the other as night from day. And *all* things which change thus into one another

or speak or understand.

It doesn't love you back.

But it is a *human* corpse.

And there are so many things you can do to it.

---

must be reduced to their matter, e.g. if from a corpse is produced an animal, the corpse is first reduced to its matter, and only then becomes an animal; and vinegar is first reduced to water, and only then becomes wine."

4

Renée Couldn't Hold It Together After All

What is holding a human together? And what kind of question is this, anyway? It's a common conception, but one much too simple, that what's holding us together on the outside is a skin suit that retains the innards. The skin suit is a fundamental aspect of our existence and not merely a vessel. But if the *whole* human is the vessel, then there's *nothing to contain*. If everything we are is part of the thing holding us together, then what is holding us together is the same as that which is contained, which is to say, whatever it is we are—but again in different words. So perhaps the question is ill-phrased.

If the question is ill-phrased, it is because the answer to the question, what is holding us together, is that there's nothing, absolutely nothing holding us together, and therefore, merely because the question is ill-phrased, we might all well fall apart.

And if we did, we might have the answer as to what it is that's holding us together.

You'd see it falling out of us between the pieces.

The question of what it is and how we might know about it, in this case, are one and the same.

All of them, who are left, are one and the same.

Each one identical to the next.

It doesn't really matter which one it is, then.

As long as it is one and the same.

Renée, for old time's sake.

She sat sunning herself on the front porch in a bikini and heart-shaped sunglasses. The patches of red fabric over her breasts and pussy squished to the adjustable minimum on the strings that connected them, acute isosceles triangles of decency, their presence meant to invoke in the viewer the idea of what if they weren't there. The day was too cold for it. When I'd moved in, she was friendly to me. We were friendly. We might have been friends. But then after a few quick conversations, that was that. If there was ever a reason for that being that, I didn't know. I made the reasonable assumption that sometimes, that's what happens. Not everyone works out. Not every relationship flourishes. How do other people know? When do we know when to stop? And imagine what it would be to know, in the moment, that this would be the last of it.

I would not become friends with Renée.

Descartes and I never got along, either.

He has this example to prove that there is something to the identity of things beyond our observation of their properties. He says in the *Meditations* that we must look to the wax. It melts, it becomes transparent, it warms, it flows, it loses its colour, liquefies—but before it melts, it is white, opaque, cool to the touch, malleable but not liquid, etc. He goes on, cataloguing its properties, as if the more disparities there are, the better the point will eventually be, because it all leads up to the twist—that before the wax melts and after, that in the process in between, *at no point,* says Descartes, does the mind ever doubt that the wax, after it has melted, is not the same wax as before.[28]

There are prima facie reasons to question this, however. For it seems, beyond a doubt, that the wax that has been melted *is certainly not* the same wax as before. The wax before, I could carry round in my pocket. The wax *before*, I could contain without containing it. The wax before did not burn me to touch it. Thus, its identity seems indeed to have altered along with the physical change.

Which is exactly as the empiricists would have it.

Oh, but we don't want to give it to *them*, either.

They would say there's nothing to the wax at all, *except* for its properties. That underneath it all, there is no *substance* to it (the word we retain for the thing that remains even if all the properties change). That all the thing is, is its properties, and to change even one of them does make it different.[29] After all, we have one

---

28   René Descartes, *Meditations on First Philosophy*, tr. Elizabeth S. Haldane, Meditation II *Of the Nature of the Human Mind; and that it is more easily known than the Body*: "Let us take, for example, this piece of wax: it has been taken quite freshly from the hive, and it has not yet lost the sweetness of the honey which it contains; it still retains somewhat of the odour of the flowers from which it has been culled; its colour, its figure, its size are apparent; it is hard, cold, easily handled, and if you strike it with the finger, it will emit a sound. Finally all the things which are requisite to cause us distinctly to recognize a body, are met with in it. But notice that while I speak and approach the fire, what remained of the taste is exhaled, the smell evaporates, the colour alters, the figure is destroyed, the size increases, it becomes liquid, it heats, scarcely can one handle it, and when one strikes it, no sound is emitted. Does the same wax remain after this change? We must confess that it remains; none would judge otherwise. What then did I know so distinctly in this piece of wax? It could certainly be nothing of all that the senses brought to my notice, since all these things which fall under taste, smell, sight, touch, and hearing, are found to be changed, and yet the same wax remains."

29   John Locke, Ibid.: "In like manner, if two or more atoms be joined together into the same mass, every one of those atoms will be the

kind of wax that is cool to the touch and another that would rip your heart out if it could.

Because that's what they do, isn't it? They're always looking to the other side of the bones to see what's back there, what they could get. This is why we must always seem solid, impenetrable, because when those semblances come into question, that's when they'll have you.

Too far. We can't infer the properties of man onto wax.

I too would burn you.

I would burn you, Renée.

We use "burn" metaphorically to mean that someone has been wronged, but also to mean someone has been insulted or otherwise made a fool of. We say, "She got burned," for instance, when whoever "she" is comes out of some deal in a less than ideal manner (perhaps she lost some money or some dignity or both). And we also say, "She got burned," when Renée makes a joke about her. I should have known. Her jokes, which seemed at the time to bring us together, like we were united in our negative opinions of an other, against whom our alliance would be tested, should have indicated to me a lower nature that would inevitably turn its attention to me. Because that's how you end up burned, by being near the fire. And while the damage to the flesh dissipates, the pain is still there.

Is it a phantom?

Is she?

After all, she could have called if she wanted.

Fuck it, burn her before she burns me.

---

same, by the foregoing rule: and whilst they exist united together, the mass, consisting of the same atoms, must be the same mass, or the same body, let the parts be ever so differently jumbled. But if one of these atoms be taken away, or one new one added, it is no longer the same mass or the same body."

If that's where the argument goes.

Keep it together.

Burn her to show that there's nothing between the parts.

Renée had a heart-shaped ass that made you want to stick your fingers in her, and she wore leggings that let you see its shape. She exercised. She had a dog. You've always got to be suspicious of women who exercise and have dogs. They've been through something. Sometimes when people get hurt, they just internalize it, until someone comes along to hurt them again. Sometimes when people get hurt, they externalize it, until someone comes along for them to hurt. Women who have dogs and exercise, they're undecided.

What about the dog?

I made plans for what I'd do with him while I texted Renée.

"It's been a minute. Coffee?"

And we wait.

The only reliable story we have of Pythagoras is that he once heard a barking dog and when the owner went to hit it, Pythagoras yelled for him to stop.[30] Because, he said, he heard in its bark the voice of a friend. He didn't mean the dog was his friend. But he did mean the dog *was his friend*. They say that a dog is man's best friend, but what Pythagoras meant, they say, is that *the soul of one of his friends was reincarnated in the dog*, and Pythagoras could recognize the friend's voice in the dog's bark. The Pythagoreans were vegetarians, because their model

---

30   "They say that, passing a belaboured whelp, He, full of pity, spake these words of dole: "Stay, smite not! 'Tis a friend, a human soul; I knew him straight when as I heard him yelp!" From the Loeb Classical Library edition of Diogenes Laertius' *Lives of Eminent Philosophers*, 8.1 Pythagoras, p. 353. The Greek reads: καί ποτέ μιν στυφελιζομένου σκύλακος παριόνταφασὶν ἐποικτῖραι καὶ τόδε φάσθαι ἔπος·"παῦσαι μηδὲ ῥάπιζ', ἐπεὶ ἦ φίλου ἀνέρος ἐστὶψυχή, τὴν ἔγνων φθεγξαμένης ἀΐων."

of reincarnation included reincarnation as animals, and you don't want to *eat* your friends.

That's too far.

Keep it together.

If the dog were Renée's friend, it wouldn't eat her, either. Why doesn't it work both ways? Why do we excuse the behaviour of my friends reincarnated as dogs, but not the people who eat them?

Let's see.

"Sure, my place?"

Renée didn't bother going out for just anyone.

I could have been anyone, but I chose to be this.

There really wasn't much to do to prepare. My equipment was already sufficient. I just needed to do the work. I needed binds (scarves for Renée) and rohypnol. I had them. I had a big purse, too.

I packed my purse and went over. I thought on the way of how it wouldn't have worked if I had asked her over to my place. She would have made some excuse. It would have nothing to do with not wanting to leave her comfort space and sit on someone else's furniture for a while. The excuse would be completely unrelated. At the same time, there was a detectable pattern, through which one could infer her true motivation—an aversion to other apartments. Some might argue that it's worse to invite someone into your own apartment. It's always the one who enters who comes off as the aggressor. *They went into her home*, they'd say. But perhaps that was the point, and I shouldn't discount that either—that Renée had a plan of her own, and that she needed her own equipment, which wasn't efficient enough to fit in a large purse, and that therefore she had to lure people over.

As I entered through the kitchen, I said hi to Charlie, the beagle.

"Charlie," I said, in a dog voice, and I rubbed his face back and forth, releasing the saliva from his floppy pink mouth in his black fur face onto my fingers. My act of defiance would be to not wipe it off on anything, like I was so used to it, I didn't have to. Like he was already my dog.

What if it didn't all come together in the end?

It's a silly question, because that assumes that you're taking a passive role in everything you do. What if it didn't come together? I'd *make it* come together. I'm not waiting for something to happen. Make it happen.

Go.

"How's your position working out for you?"

"Oh, you know," I said. "The administration can be difficult."

She looked at me like it was an opportunity for an argument. But she wasn't aware that none of the arguments were relevant any longer. She was hoping I would defend a position I in fact no longer held, because of some upper administrative movements that had led us both here. That, and I think she was always suspicious of me.

"You're sure it's not anything you've done," she intimated. *You're sure*, she said, as if to make it about my belief about what happened and not about what actually happened. She did not know what happened.

"Sure," I confirmed, perhaps agreed. Sometimes you have to agree, just because you know someone will be dead soon, and it all won't have mattered.

We went on and on about jobs, men, sexual partners, where we'd lived, what we'd done, what had been done to us, as if we were revealing our secrets, but we weren't really. It was a talking match, where every problem was revealed in the best possible light and every insight had already been repeated so often it sounded like a script written for genre fiction, satisfaction coming only when each party successfully played out their role as caricature. Is this what people do? Talk like this to death?

Yes.

Kill them.

I offered to get the coffee from the kitchen. She wouldn't stop me. It would be too much to stop me, out of rhythm. But this is how we who deviate establish the opportunity to deviate—by relying on the immutable habits of others. I doubled her dose to counteract the coffee, but uppers don't cancel out downers, so I wasn't worried about them not working. If anything, they enhance them. Maybe she would be a happier person in an hour.

But she wouldn't drink it. It was some sort of personal rebellion, either at my arguments or because I'd fetched it and therefore it had been sullied, and all this despite the fact that she'd brought me here, over here, all the way over here, and I decided she must have done so, because she thought she was in control of this space and of all of the things in it, and she wanted me to be one of those things, but I wouldn't.

Just don't.

As I was thinking of more ways to argue in favor of my overall claim that faculty are the only necessary part of a university, I noticed that any further arguments would be wasted, for Renée had replaced responses with nods, slow nods, nods of agreement or nods that were meant to stave off unconsciousness, it didn't matter. I'd already won the argument. Renée had drunk the dose. Forfeit, reason of unconsciousness.

"Let's go to bed," I said, and she nodded again.

I walked over to her side of the room and offered her my

hand. When she didn't take it, I grabbed her elbow and used that to hoist her up to a standing position, putting myself under her shoulder in the most stable configuration I could conceive. I walked her some too many intoxicated half steps to the bedroom and laid her down on her side, then went back for my purse. Something told me she bought a bed with posts just to be tied down to it, that it was a sign of sorts. I wouldn't put it past her to have known that this was coming, I was coming, and here we are.

The present decided long in the past.

It doesn't matter, anymore.

I took off her shirt as if I were helping her to undress, then I bound her left wrist to the bedpost while she raised her right hand in the air, as if asking permission to raise a question. "What's that?" she asked me, as I took the arm from the air and leaned over her, tying it to the other post with another scarf, all gifts unenthusiastically received, biding their time in the closet at home until the moment Renée had to be restrained. I thought it added a personal touch.

"To stop you from moving," I said, and she nodded.

I peeled off her leggings and smelled the spot where her pussy had been. They weren't synthetic, of course, so the smell was enhanced by the fabric. I looped the fabric around my neck, balancing the weight to keep the scent in place on my chest, where normally I would have applied perfume.

Her pussy was different than mine, and I mean that in the most basic and literal sense, in that it was all there was to say. It was another pussy, one that wasn't mine. There was nothing magic about it. Renée didn't ask questions when I tied the scarves around on her ankles, she just made a little sound, like she knew what I was doing and that it was for her own good.

She was wearing black panties with sheer panels on the side, and her bra matched, of course. I stuck a finger in her pussy, in through the side of her panties, the nylon frictionless, as though it were designed not to impede penetration. On the one hand, I resented her for wearing nicer things than I did, because I knew that it mattered. On the other hand, I felt bad that she thought she had to do it all the time—the habit was so internalized that she had to wear nice underthings, even just to have coffee with a friend, in her own apartment. I thought of her on the porch in her bikini, who it might be for, but it was no one. No one actual. If woman has but a relative existence, her rebellion can take the form of relative existence for its own sake. In my speculations, Renée dressed in a way men would like just to deny herself to them. Like making someone their favourite food and then throwing it in the trash.

I put my finger in my mouth, just to wet it, and then back inside. I went up and down, side to side, as if trying to find something that wasn't there, something that explained why anyone would be so engrossed by this bit of anatomy, but all there was, was flesh, and nothing more. Renée wriggled a little as I moved around, and then I got it, the inexplicable surge and urge to fuck something, the tangible change in how my blood circulated, the contradictory perceptions of affect and lack, like an ungrounded current moving through my clit that threatened to disperse when it wanted resolve, a sensation that demanded more sensation.

And we're the only ones here.

I moved my hand from Renée's pussy to mine, rubbing the clitoris and surrounding area side to side until I came without satisfaction. There was something about doing it with nothing inside that meant less. I looked around Renée's room for something to fuck her with. She lay there with her eyes closed, waiting. I found a ceramic figurine of a woman, all white and delicate, hollow inside, with a mark on the bottom to indicate its respectable origin, and whether it was a gift or something someone had given her, I felt like this woman was supposed to represent her, be a smaller version of her, emphasize her qualities by reproducing them in miniature, and it seemed vain to keep it out like that, a better, smaller, more breakable version of herself. Like how she would always artificially raise her voice to seem smaller and more fragile.

If I were going to fuck her with it, I'd have to gag her.

I brought extra materials in case of unanticipated situations, and this seemed like one of them. I made a gag out of a counterfeit Hermes and tied it all the way around her head. If I just balled it in her mouth, it might come out. Any attempt to escape should instead ensure its efficiency. So all the way around it went. All the way around, and then with my right hand moving on her clit, I took the figurine and put it in her mouth, behind the gag. The look on her face was indignant, like the click of the ceramic against her teeth foretold the end of a good time. And then I broke it.

With my right hand still going and her stuck in position, Renée tried not to swallow any of its sharpness and failed. It's funny what sorts of poisons one can encounter. It's not that this was bad for her, but only because of its shape, and its shape was its shape only by chance. I had control over the fact that it would break, but not into what shape it might, and in the end, it's the particular shape that matters. Nothing held it together.[31] Her sounds were high and tight, like she was trying to close her

---

31 Someone and their image are in fact not similar; we cannot say of both Simmias and his image that "It's Simmias." Cf. Plato's argument from recollection in the *Phaedo* and, in particular, 73d-e. The incongruity is illustrated best by Magritte in his *La Trahison des images*.

throat and failing. I imagined the pieces making their way inside, changing her constitution, making her something other than she was. On the premise of materialism, Renée was constituted of her own organic substance. On the premise of functionalism, she was the network of activities that her individual body performed in the fulfillment of its *telos*. Full of piercing ceramic pieces defying the body's mechanisms, Renée would be something other than she was on either account.

She was almost unrecognizable already, her face contorted due to being in a situation in which she did not want to be, her makeup draining over it to form a caricature, a mask of what a human might be, an uncanny resemblance of woman that revealed its fragility. Still, if at this point someone were to find the body and if someone else were to ask, "Is this Renée?" all but a very stupid individual or perhaps someone who didn't know her might say, "Yes." I would be very clever and point out to them that no, it wasn't, because the Renée you knew *wasn't full of ceramic pieces*. The Reneé you knew's insides were not all torn up by them! And they would smile and say, of course. Because of the requirements for persistent identity over time of a material object according to empiricism! And then we would both laugh.

I went back for my purse.

Inside was a vial of sodium hydroxide in crystal form. (It was that or the micro pearls; I chose the one with edges.) Renée's material transformation can't simply be the integration of foreign material. Her own material must change. Otherwise, you might remove the ceramic parts and say she was once again the same (once the wounds had healed, *if* they would). The point is, the integration of foreign materials is itself not a chemical change that ensures her own materiality is altered. *There are some chemical changes that are only theoretically reversible,* unlike some other physical changes, and that's what the corrosive is for. And there's a paperweight on the desk that seems about right, from some local glass shop that made them just for the poor tourists who couldn't afford the nice pieces. Oblong, the colours inside formed a helix, while the bubbles added refraction and demonstrated the item's artisan origin.

A small vial, and thin, like a perfume sample. Like one of those tiny bottles of ginseng you were supposed to take every day to improve your memory, if only you could stomach the taste. Weird saying that—you weren't really stomaching the taste, you were mouthing it, and stomaching the nutrient. A good thing. But we don't talk about stomaching things that are good, and that's very strange. I put the vial in her pussy and pushed it in with my fingers.

I pushed the paperweight in afterward. There must, I determined, be some finite amount of pressure one might exert against the thin glass of the vial before it broke, and I did not want to get its contents on my hands. Using the heavier glass weight as hammer, I rammed the oval into her, again and again, changing angles as her pain increased and her groaning intensified until, gagged or not, ceramic bits or not, Renée tried to scream, and I knew that the chemical was working. I pictured her cervix dissolving, filling the void with liquid flesh produced of the reaction. *If soap comes out, that means that pussy was FAT!* I laughed. I empathetically reproduced the sensation, like someone ejaculating fire into her. Of course, I couldn't feel it and wouldn't want to. Some things are better imagined. The screaming took me out of the situation a little, as I had to put up a block in my consciousness to tolerate the sound. No hint of any falsetto now, although perhaps if she'd thought of it she might have considered the neighbours would be more likely to hear her in a higher tone of voice, the theoretical reason why adults are attracted to the high-pitched voices of children, or rather, why we aver them. The sound is *horrid*.

Renée gave up screaming and took up crying, and it all must have been very confusing, because she wasn't all there to begin with and couldn't possibly understand what was going on. The material change I'd introduced would be invisible, if the chemical stayed contained and only did internal damage. If you melted the inside of a candle without doing any discernible damage to the outside, you might never know. Does its identity persist?

How far did we have to go to make sure Renée isn't what she was?

That's where Charlie must play a role. The dog. My new dog and research assistant.

I realized Renée wasn't helping us anymore, so I held a pillow over her face for a very, very long time. They don't show you how long it takes, usually, when such acts are represented on films or TV. They don't show you the pillow isn't what's suffocating her. It's me. The pillow just fills in the gaps that I can't possibly hold together on my own, not all at once. It's a tool—a big, fluffy hand to condense against someone. But you've got to stay there, on the other side, not letting the air through as best you can. Luckily, people need a lot of air to live and not just a little, otherwise she'd just wait there for me to let go and then pop up again. *Aha! Tricked you!* she'd say. *Yes, I thought you were dead again*, I'd say, we'd laugh, and then we'd go back to our positions.

When that was done, I went into the kitchen for some instruments I was sure Renée would have. The large knife was easy to find. As she'd joked when I'd come into the apartment this evening, she did believe that even though she didn't cook, a kitchen counter didn't look right without a set of knives. The vessel was harder. She didn't think that pots and pans were things you needed just for show. I found a twelve-inch unseasoned cast iron pan in the bottom drawer that, I imagine, someone must have given her. That's fine. In fact, better. The lingering remains of old food wouldn't alter her taste and sully the experiment.

I cut the boneless parts off first, seared the meat and let it come to temperature. I thought Charlie would balk at eating her raw. Maybe when he got used to the taste, he'd do it, but at first I thought he might appreciate my making her more like the canned mush to which he was already accustomed. I took everything out of the refrigerator, even the shelves. *No one is recognizable in very small parts.* It's odd that Descartes didn't think it fit to mention that. What happens to something's identity when it's *in parts* is a whole other question. It's outside the scope of this study. Something for a later time, perhaps. I put her body in the fridge, besides the parts I cooked, which I took from unnoticeable places. I gave Charlie his meal, patted him on the head and washed up. It's important to stay tidy in the lab, and the lab is wherever I'm working, so I suppose that means it's here.

Twice a day, I would come by, take Charlie outside, open the fridge and record his reaction. He was the perfect little subject, I thought, because his judgement of something's identity wouldn't be clouded by the same old habitual concepts we have, where things tend to remind us of things that they aren't, and where we want to believe things continue to exist when they don't. Charlie wouldn't have all that to deal with, so we could trust his judgement and his appetite. Day after day went by like that. On the street, people recognized Charlie, and I let them have a pat at him. I didn't mention that by this point he'd be twenty-five, fifty, sixty-five percent human by volume. They didn't seem to notice. Perhaps souls are not consumed after all.

Every time I opened the refrigerator, Charlie winced, looking at the eyes and pawing at the ground, as if waiting for her to rise. I'd lock him in the bedroom when I took another part away, to see how much would have to go before, to Charlie, she became someone else. She was dead to me before this whole thing started, so my opinion didn't count. One day, I heard the whining in his voice change from recognition to hunger, the excitement of anticipating the affection of a loved one replaced by a merely mechanical indication of emptiness, and I knew Renée was gone. Had her soul been transferred with the meat to Charlie? A form of reincarnation, certainly, but the material not the soul, and we all know that way doesn't count. Besides, I could finally take my dog home, and I didn't want her coming along with us.

Now at no point could I discern what it was that held a human identity together, and while I could conclude that it was nothing, that would only replicate the arrogant conclusions of the empiricists. Because there are things that we cannot see. Nevertheless, the experiment wasn't without purpose, because now if anyone asks how long it takes for someone to undo, to turn from someone into no one, to become nothing from something, and to all together not hold together, I can tell them with some certainty that it's eleven and one-half days.

5

Ode to Dora (The Case Study of Sigmund)

Dora, whose case study Freud wrote on the topic of hysteria (name changed to protect the privacy of Ida Bauer). Dora, the neurotic whose voice might never return, except through the application of an old man's cock to her throat. Dora, who said "no" and was labeled a hysteric for it. Hysteria, the disease named for the uterus and as a catch-all descriptor for any such disorder as anyone with said uterus might dream up.

Dora said "no." She said "no" to Herr K. and "no" to Herr Freud too. She said "no" to the cock and "no" to the hysteria, and now we all know, Dora, what it is you didn't do.

Dora who was accused of lying by her father. Dora who was dropped off to Dr. Freud to cure her of her neuroses, which Dr. Freud attributes to her secret desire to suck Herr K's old cock. Dora, whom he called hysterical for her refusal to do it. Dora, whose only insanity was "no," "no" to the cocks of old men, and Dora of whom the good doctor said, "I should without question consider a person hysterical in whom an occasion for sexual excitement elicited feelings that were preponderantly or exclusively unpleasurable."[32] Dora, whose symptoms were, "dyspnoea, tussis nervosa, aphonia, and possibly migraines, together with depression, hysterical unsociability, and a taedium vitae which was probably not entirely genuine."[33] Dora, who left the good doctor after only three months' treatment, and Dora, whom Freud decided must have left because she recognized a secret love for doctor cock and couldn't handle the implications.

Dora who cannot escape the cocks.

Who's crazy just for trying.

After all, a good cock just might fix the problem.

So too the ancients had said.

In the ancient cases of hysteria (and get off my fucking back you pedants who insist that hysteria is a modern disease whose name just happens to be based on the Greek word *hysteros*, because I don't give a flying iota), the cause was known to be the dislodgement of the uterus (*hysteros*) and its subsequent wandering around the torso, searching for its proper home. Hysteria which was really "hysterical suffocation," because the uterus would exert pressure wherever it was in the body that it shouldn't be, and whose cause was that the patient was too cold and wet and altogether unfucked. The patient whose uterus must be lured back to its place by the application of something warm and dry. A good dicking. So says Hippocrates in *On the Diseases of Women* I.7, and we should all believe him, because he also wrote the oath.

Hysteria was removed from the Diagnostic and Statistical

---

32   Herr Doktor Freud's case study, *Fragment of an Analysis of a Case of Hysteria*, better known as *Dora*, recently translated again as *A Case of Hysteria (Dora)* with a painting of a very young woman on the cover, pretending to be modest even though you can tell she wants to get fucked hard.

33   And again.

Manual of Mental Disorders in 1980, when all of a sudden it came to light that a disease was invented by doctors whose prescribed treatment was dick (quite possibly doctor dick).

Freud *did not* say the physical cause of Dora's aphonia was that her uterus had moved up there to suffocate her, and that's medical progress for sure. Also, on the Hippocratic account of hysterical suffocation, the dick should be applied to the vagina. But Freud thought that face fucking might be the key to Dora's issue. So, certainly, these are very different diseases with very different treatments. In fact, if one were to treat an ancient case of hysteria with cock sucking, the theoretical end result is that the uterus might just end up in a woman's neck or face. And wouldn't that be embarrassing. It is of the utmost importance, then, for the sake of medical science, that the dick be applied as prescribed.

A Fragment of an Analysis of a Case Study of Sigmund

For the purpose of this case study, I have changed the name of my subject (object?) in order to preserve his privacy. He is a well-known member of the local psychological community, more so for his transgressions than his research. He remains employed by the university by whom I was recently employed, despite those transgressions. (You may know him as that professor who is forbidden to hire female teaching assistants).

"Sigmund" was committed to my care for three months, and unfortunately his case remains unresolved. Nevertheless, the details of his neurosis, treatment and eventual death must be of some importance to posterity. I therefore report, as faithfully as possible, the details which I believe to be relevant to the disciplines interested in this case. Sigmund was involuntarily transported to the laboratory under a chemically-induced slumber to avoid the trauma we might witness in persons who are forcibly removed from any one circumstance and placed in an all together different one. Waking peacefully in another environment, it was almost possible to convince the subject he had always been there, and his previous life had been a dream or some other such hallucination. (This effect wore off as treatment continued, and Sigmund came to long for his previous life, such that his positive valuation of his former circumstance lent credulity to its existence. That is to say, the more he wanted to go home, the more he was sure that such a home had actually existed.)

I have observed Sigmund for some time in professional settings, and it is clear he suffers from a severe form of delusion that impacts both his professional and personal lives. The delusion is peculiar for its recognizable falsehood. Sigmund believes the world is inhabited by people numbering only half of the census tallies—any individual he perceives to be female (according to his own definition of femininity) simply does not count. In any given situation, Sigmund will behave as if half of the individuals present either do not exist at all, or do not exist in any meaningful way. (He will not engage with them on an intellectual level.) At times, Sigmund's delusion leads him to believe in a sort of grandeur such that half of the population, due to their irreality, owes him their servitude. (Once at an academic conference, I witnessed him turn to another colleague and ask her to please fetch him a cup of tea, "won't you, dear.") This delusion is particularly nefarious, as his confidence in it leads others around him to believe in it as well, even some of those members of the population whom Sigmund has designated unreal. It is therefore imperative that Sigmund be cured of it, with haste, and privately, so that in the midst of his treatment, Sigmund might not seek social reinforcement of his delusion from peers who have humoured him in the past.

The particularity of the condition introduced a barrier to my treatment's efficacy early on, as upon Sigmund's waking in the laboratory, it quickly became clear I would first have to convince Sigmund of my own personhood, before treatment could begin. His words, "What have you done, you bitch!" indicated he was lost to his delusion and that he cognized me, a former colleague, not as human at all, but perhaps animal or some other entity unworthy of respectful treatment. Because of how ingrained his delusion had come to be, I realized I would have to at once convince him that I, too, was human, and thinking quickly, I imagined what, according the rules of his delusion, a human might do. And so I punched him in the nose. (This is why, throughout the treatment, the patient complained incessantly about the ongoing pain of an unset break; however, I do not believe the fracture impacted his progress.) Nevertheless, no treatment is without some detriment, and it is often reported that pain is part of the therapeutic process and necessary to the success of the treatment. It is therefore recommended the therapist inure herself to these and other such cries of pain to which, if one were to respond in an empathetic manner, would derail the patient's progress and quite possibly negate any chance of future rehabilitation, once the patient recognizes the power their pain has over the therapist's own behaviour. I, for one, am completely at ease with the repercussions of this perhaps unorthodox start to our treatment, as had I done anything else, the path to recovery might never have begun.

Because of this early treatment intervention, Sigmund at once perceived the power dynamic between us, and that, along with how I'd removed his freedom to move his arms and legs (through the application of dollar store zip ties), he was perhaps on the subordinate end of that relation. By encouraging this conception,

I was hoping he would, by means of some inferred authority, lend me the authority also of personhood. (If he is subordinate to me, it is because my opinions are authoritative; if my opinions are authoritative, it is because I am human.) Thus, my ongoing restraint of the patient and his subsequent treatment involved methods meant to humiliate him both mentally and physically, such that he might become accustomed to his subordinate position and thus work toward ridding himself of his delusion.

It is my belief the patient ultimately wanted to be cured, and would therefore have supported my treatment of him, if not for the immediate pain it caused. But the therapist must keep this in mind, as no uttered assertion of the patient would ever support it. Instead, Sigmund continued to curse at me for several days, while I repeated to him, "If you curse at me, you certainly find me a being worthy of cursing. I am a human." To which he would respond, "You're a bitch," which I took to be evidence of denial, first of my treatment but ultimately of the disease. (It is never the case that a patient remains deluded, having been truly convinced of their delusion. The application of rationality to the delusion does not mitigate its persistence; it is only by the persistent efforts of rehabituating the patient to an alternative conceptual framework that such a delusion might be cured.)

At this point, I must convey to the reader how entrenched these delusions might become, if left to fester over years or even decades. The patient is willing to deny their very perceptions, if only the delusion might be maintained. In the case of Sigmund, he was eventually able to recognize all of the human qualities I embodied—rationality, agency, freedom of will, the capacity to express myself in a language constructed of grammatical elements combined to indicate states of the soul—and one might think that having perceived those qualities, he might make the inference that I am human. But the patient is not rational. He is diseased, and the disease will make every effort to survive. Thus, through logical manipulations, the patient was never completely rid of his delusion that half of perceived humans were inhuman, despite having learned over the course of treatment that his conception of these non-humans was *incorrect*. To Sigmund, the idea that "women are human" was possible to hold in the abstract, but never could he recognize any instances of its truth from within his own viewpoint in reality.

When Sigmund began his treatment, he would utter nonsensical declarative statements like, "women are so emotional." This statement and others of the sort were meant to differentiate between women and "real humans" by virtue that real humans were *not* so emotional while women *were*. After several sessions, Sigmund admitted that a similar amount of emotional expression/experience was common to both "women" and "real humans," but this would alter his definition of what it meant to be a "real human"—an alteration meant to ensure that half the population would again be excluded from his definition of "humanity." (A real human doesn't menstruate; a real human's centre of gravity is slightly higher; a real human naturally commands a certain authority, etc. He would say anything to avoid collapsing the classes of real and unreal humans into one.) Our treatments carried on in such fashion until, near the end, Sigmund could find no distinguishing feature between what his delusion told him were the real humans and the unreal ones, except those very qualities—that of all the humans, some were "real," and others were "unreal." Sigmund maintained that the distinction would remain true, even if he was the only person alive who could recognize the differences he saw to be inherent. (He might even have taken pride in the idea that he would have such special powers.)

The truth of the matter was, though he would never admit to it, Sigmund thought rationality was housed in the cock. This is why he conceives the appendage as worthy of envy. And of course, I did want one. Not for anything else but for fucking. It seemed fortuitous to have one in certain situations, but one comes to recognize over time that it isn't the cock that lends its bearer the authority on so many matters. It's not the cock that guarantees a man is getting the respect he "deserves." No one ever checks, in fact, what is inside the pants of anyone else, except very rarely, and not with that intent in mind. Rather, the genitals are inferred from another set of behaviours, including manners of dress and adornment, which one might manipulate to *infer* the preferred genitalia, if one were so stuck on the idea that it was the genitalia that mattered, but again, it really does not. The concepts of man and woman have become so untethered from sex organs that it really does seem possible, at the moment of writing, that I might command a masculine level of respect from a colleague even without it.

That is to say, while I understand why a "woman" might envy someone with a penis, it's not for the sake of the genitalia itself, but for all of the attendant social structures that benefit a person with that genitalia. It's not penis envy at all; it's envy of the respect and authority to which it seems the bearer of the penis is entitled.

A cock for fucking, on the other hand, you can just buy at the store.

Which is what I did, for Sigmund.

Because I believe that, with the appropriate application of the treatment I envisioned, Sigmund might come to empathize along with those who, from his entrenched vantage point, are not just fucked, but exist *for* fucking.

Let him live for it too, then.

Let him live through it.

Or not.

All treatments come with risk.

At first, the treatment suffered from two setbacks, one mental and one physical. Because of the patient's resistance to admit there was a disease, the efficacy of treatment might at first have been diminished, as it is very important in the psychological realm for the patient first to admit there is a problem to treat. The human mind will otherwise set up all sorts of barriers in order to maintain a sort of mental inertia—the ability to continue working with defective forms of thought and consciousness, despite all evidence that these forms of thought and consciousness are, in fact, defective. The other barrier to treatment was physical. As Sigmund was not born with a vaginal opening, it had to be created, to administer his treatment in the manner prescribed by ancient and modern sciences.

To create Sigmund's vaginal opening, I sought out a cutting implement equal in breadth to the cock which I ultimately intended to apply. Because the flesh is pliable, the measurements need not be too specific. It is natural to experience some tearing, if an enthusiastic therapist applies a treatment to an unprepared orifice. Because of Sigmund's psychological resistance to the treatment, I decided to cut, instead of just one hole, many. I inserted the implement into the flesh but, because the cutting implement is flat and the treatment implement cylindrical, I found it necessary to turn the knife one hundred and eighty degrees after insertion, in order to admit the sort of cylindrical object the treatment demanded.

I positioned Sigmund's "vaginal" openings in the pelvis, above his own genitals. I made cuts under his arms, where the treatment might lead to a change of heart and, turning him over, manufactured two more holes up through his buttocks. These were unique, as they admitted both entrance and exit of the implements, and they would, throughout the treatment, heal to some degree. Like a massive piercing, the body would attempt to form a skin tube from one end to the other. To counteract its urge to heal, I had to ensure some of the treatments conducted were more vigourous at times, ensuring the new flesh could never take hold. To close the wounds would be to render the openings inefficacious. Sealed with flesh, they wouldn't provide the kind of wounds I wanted Sigmund to have—raw, constant, vulnerable to all forms of environmental irritant. I wanted him at the mercy of the air.

At first, I would fuck Sigmund's holes intermittently, believing as I had been told by medical science that to replicate the physical act of love would be sufficient to treat his condition. While this was somewhat effective, it did not entirely rid the subject of his delusions. (When I say it was "somewhat effective," I mean this form of treatments successfully cured the patient of his *taedium vitae* (weariness of life), a well-known symptom of hysteria, though by no means the defining symptom. What this indicated is that the diagnosis was correct, and the treatment was indeed working, but Sigmund's case had developed so far beyond the case studies present in the literature, that he required an advanced form of treatment based on the same principles.) Thus, I acquired implements whose motions were self-propelled, so that I could continue work on my other research. I increased the number of his vaginal openings from five to nine—inserting the knife as previously specified through the thighs, then, discovering those openings not to be near enough the subject's vital organs to occasion a change of heart, created two more openings under the ribcage. Because these were near to the viscera (a necessity of the treatment), I inserted the knife superficially, and then relied on the prosthetic dicks to complete the work of not only filling but creating the void, bluntly and without risk of puncturing Sigmund's lungs.

As the vibrating cocks sometimes became loose of their own accord, I restrained them in position using whatever was available at the time, while paying the utmost attention to the sanitary conditions of Sigmund's wounds. While the vaginal opening is naturally self-cleaning, Sigmund's artificial ones were not. Thus, he required the attentive care of a nurse as well as a therapist, and the treatment soon came to occupy so much of my time that I felt rather overcommitted through those final weeks. I recommend to any other therapist engaging in such a course of treatment that they acquire an assistant first, before the treatment itself monopolizes the time it would take to do so later on.

No matter how many times I raped Sigmund, he never came to enjoy it. His own genitals hung, limp and useless, and he had trouble maintaining an erection, even as I told him how he should be enjoying the act of love he was enduring. If he enjoyed it, he would be cured. After all, "I should without question consider a person hysterical in whom an occasion for sexual excitement elicited feelings that were preponderantly or exclusively unpleasurable."[34] With such resistance on the part of the patient, it was not a surprise when the treatment ultimately failed. As a final escalation of my methods, I created one final orifice under Sigmund's chin and, applying the treatment as near to the source of the issue as possible, saw in his eyes how stubbornly he held to his delusions, even as death overwhelmed him.

---

34 Recall the good doctor, above.

Interim discussion: Repetition as a Defining Characteristic of Philosophy as a Rigorous Science: The Time After Time[35]

Time doesn't pass in the dark.

Although, I do wish it would.

Wouldn't it be nice if the world were dying outside?

To wake up to nothing.

The framework of experimentation demanded we identify a "before" and an "after," that the "before" be obliterated in face of the "after," which when all is said and done, becomes its own kind of "before."

It was all so exhausting.

There is no time after time.

Time after time after time after time until no time at all.

Time is the number of change, and change necessitates movement.[36]

Movement requires a direction.

Direction requires an end.

The end is built in.

---

35 Cf. Edmund Husserl, "*Philosophie als strenge Wissenschaft*" (*Logos I*, 1911, S. 289-341).

36 Cf. Aristotle's *Physics*.

It's over.

Repetition is an imitation of eternity.[37]

I'm not the only one who's been victimized by time.

When time is over, the pain should stop, too.

But not all pains have sources.

Some sources are dead, but the pains remain.

Burns and wounds and loneliness.

A sense that something is wrong and it's staying that way.

That to which we become accustomed.

Cioran talks about the fall out of time as a darkness that becomes a living death; the subject as onlooker observes through a lens of non-wants. The lack of any desire directed toward future existence and the present, constitutes a lack of time itself. The future is the lack of the present, where desire is all around. Desire is desire because of a lack the present doesn't fulfill. The future is the future, because it is the end of our desires and the fulfillment of the present's lack. Where there is no desire, there is no future, and thus there is the fall out of time. Negative eternity.[38]

But what of dread?

What of the structureless desire for what is gone and lost?

Desire is only future-oriented if linear time is the thing, always moving forward, always a gain. Something that wasn't becomes and then is, or we want it to be.

---

37 Cf. Plato's *Timaeus*.

38 "The eternity that set itself above time gives way to that other eternity which lies beneath, a sterile zone where I can desire only one thing: to reinstate time, to get back into it at any price, to appropriate a piece of it, to give myself the illusion of a place of my own. But time is sealed off, time is out of reach; and it is the impossibility of penetrating it which constitutes this negative eternity, this *wrong* eternity." Emil Cioran, *The Fall Into Time*, tr. Richard Howard (Chicago: Quadrangle Books, 1970), p. 174.

But what of the something that is, but then wasn't?

How do I want that, and so badly?

So badly.

So badly.

"That's irrational," they'll say. As if rationality were the future term we all want.

I used to take a Xanax before every class. I thought I'd get over the anxiety sometime over those many years, but I never did. It doesn't mean I don't like teaching. There's still a way to do it so that everyone will love you.

And isn't that the goal?

Take the best parts of every professor you know, and then update that to correspond to how people are raised now, then relate to them like a fucking human might, then they all might love you.

Me.

At the end, I knew it was the end, but the trick is not to say anything about it.

It's all out of place as it happens.

At the end of the semester, they will all forget my name, but I'll be thinking about them forever.

I probably cried in the car on the way to work.

I probably wrote down something about suicide.

Until I figured out that depression constitutes a disindividuation. And by that, I mean it makes everyone who suffers it think the same old thoughts. It takes away your individuality and dissipates your personhood, until all that's left is the time after time and no one to live through it.

Suffer through it.

Pathemata mathemata.

There are two forms of eternity, and you can't reach one of

them by negating yourself.

There's a disindividuation in the sense of becoming universal.

And there's a disindividuation in the sense of becoming nothing—not becoming, the failure to become.

That's what the negative eternity is.

You can't supersede your own subjectivity by becoming less than a subject.

Suicide isn't the overcoming of human finitude.

It's giving up your finitude, when it's all that you've got left.

Become a God some other way, you fuck.

6

On the Feed and Fuck Model of Happiness and its Inadequacy as a Strategic Priority (John)

The problem with trying to do philosophy within the institution is its administration. There's a tendency because of reduced government funding to direct the institution toward a business model, a profitability model, where students are clients instead of knowledge seekers, where faculty are a product to be sold at a profit and not its foundation. The whole set up is a blow to the face of Plato's Academy. The ideal city does not confuse merchants with philosophers.

Humanity is meant for something more than profitable exchanges.

Trends are toward the destruction of the humanities on the national level.

Don't you know you need me?

You need to me to let you out of the cave.

You need me to tell you that there is one.

You need me to inform you that you live there.

You need me, because all of the light is outside.

But there you are, in Plato's cave.

Looking at the shadows on the wall.[39]

Trying to put them together in such a way that the budget will come out in the black.

It shouldn't be that hard; it's all black in there.

Form your arguments to appeal to their economic mindsets, they said.

But the economic mindset is the problem.

It's the soul's misguided attachment to the body that makes it privilege the economic.

It's the failure of thought to do so.

To make thought a slave of the economic.

To think that thought is meant only to feed.

To enslave the soul to the body.

Feed and fuck and feed and fuck, so says the economic model.

They yell it from the cave and demand I go down with them.

Explain it to them in a way that makes sense.

Using only the shadows.

As if it is a privilege to join them there.

Make my arguments to be allowed back down.

How many fucks will your arguments feed?

The red and the black are mere colours. *The light itself is what*

---

39   Plato, *Republic*, 514a-b: "Next, I said, compare the effect of education and of the lack of it on our nature to an experience like this: Imagine human beings living in an underground, cavelike dwelling, with an entrance a long way up, which is both open to the light and as wide as the cave itself. They've been there since childhood, fixed in the same place, with their necks and legs fettered, able to see only in front of them, because their bonds prevent them from turning their heads around. Light is provided by a fire burning far above and behind them. Also behind them, but on higher ground, there is a path stretching between them and the fire. Imagine that along this path a low wall has been built, like the screen in front of puppeteers above which they show their puppets."

shines. But they don't see the light, they only see the colours it illuminates, and the colours represent numbers, which represent the feedings they expect to distribute amongst themselves. *If it weren't for the light, you wouldn't see the colours at all!* I scream at them. But they laugh and say, *What light? There's no light, silly woman. The colours are all that there is to see. If there were such a thing as light, make it appear to us as a colour! Then we shall see it! Oh, you cannot? Then the failure is yours! Leave this cave and all that's in it. It's ours to feed in and to fuck!*

If you only knew how you need me.

You will know how you need me.

You will know how to need me.

Today we test the business model of human happiness.

We will see how you do without the light.

How the colours appear in the dark.

Whether you can survive on the economic feed and fuck model where the only known reward is blackness.

Can you?

For how long?

The feed and fuck model of eternity is by nature finite (and therefore contradictory), for no man has ever escaped death by feeding and fucking. *To move beyond those things*, beyond the confines of the material body, and into the realm of thought, is your only hope now. *Outside the cave*, the feed and fuck model of life will appear as a dream, a former existence in which you had become so ensconced, your thoughts manipulated toward a false God. And I—I shall appear as epiphany, as the inhabitants of Plato's cave turn from the wall and see the fires that set the shadows upon their walls.

I am the fire as well.

You shall see, John, how the red and the black appear in the darkness.

Thou shalt not, John, fail to notice the fire.

And you shall never—*ever*—leave the cellar, because how easy it is to forget what one has learned and resume one's old habits, once the immediate threat of the fire has gone. If there's any saving you now, it's to live the rest of your existence in this cave that I designed, to keep the fire burning, to let you one day see it, but not now.

Not today.

Today, like every other day, we must emphasize the inadequacy of the feed and fuck model of the good life.

It was easy to get John into the cellar. He was so concerned about everything he was to lose that he went in on his own. For all of what he'd gone through already, he was certainly confident that he had retained the upper hand. Men in power always assume that—that their power transcends their realm of affect. This is why they adopt an intimidating air, so that even at the grocery store, people over whom they have no direct influence can still feel their power. But power is an interesting thing. There are so many preconditions to its existence, that it seems miraculous they should all come together at all. In order to be in power, someone must be born. They must be in the right place at the right time, in so many places and at so many times that somehow, as if by accident, here they are, floating to the top of some socially constructed institution, the existence of which also seems miraculous, when you think about how many things had to happen just right, like the parts of the human body working in harmony. *How easy it is to get wrong*. But here John was, confident in his superiority and also in the idea that *no one could just take it from him and lock him in a cellar*.

Now you might argue that he didn't get there at all by

accident, that he was in fact thrust toward a position of power by his birth, his upbringing, his privilege, and I'd have to agree with you there. And yet at the same time, through all of the social structures working to his benefit and also to the detriment of so many others, he had to *remain alive*, which itself is difficult. When at any time, any one at all could have jammed a fork in his neck and ended it. I'd thought about it myself, of course, but what would that prove? Only the futility of existence in the face of human freedom.

How many acts of violence weren't committed, just by accident?

We make it seem as if it were a choice.

But the fact is, no one's thought of it.

John's still here, because it simply hadn't occurred to anyone to stop his life from happening.

Or it had, and as per usual, John relied on the invisible forcefield of his birth and his position, as if it provided a suit of armour against possible threats. *But these things are all invisible*, you know. There is no forcefield; there is no physical distinction between the killable members of our population and the unkillable ones. Even though it seems that some sorts of individuals are more taken to victimization than others, if there's one lesson I want you to take home from John's experiment, is that *you can kill absolutely anyone you want*.

All people are potentially dead.

Interred in materiality, the force fields emanate. It's an alternative form of survival, where one comes to consider not merely the necessities of life but what it takes to flourish. We can't kill John, they'll say, in case we need him. We can't kill John, because incarceration would stymy the plans we have for the future. We can't kill John, because the meat would be bloated with fat, and the nutrition he might provide has all been pissed away, replaced with a sense of righteousness and "doing what he had to do" that would surely do detriment to those who would consume him. But when the institutions fall apart, the force fields fall with it, and the reasons we can't kill John become merely psychological, reflecting nothing in the external world. *Nothing but an unhealthy habit keeps him alive now.*

John is meat like the rest of them.

"You can't put me down here," he said, walking down anyway.

"It's not against policy," I responded, mocking his official statements.

"Your career will never recover from this, I'll make sure of that," he threatened, descending the wooden staircase to the dirt floor below.

It's weird how people who don't do any physical labour believe that "making sure" is actually a form of work. *That's not how it works, John.* When someone does the work and someone else "makes sure" it is done, only one person has done anything. And it wasn't you, John.

You'll make sure of nothing, John. You'll make sure of nothing ever again.

The business model of human happiness demanded I feed and fuck John for as long as it took. To what? It wasn't clear. I knew he wouldn't come around to an alternative view, so that couldn't be the goal. There wasn't any sort of hypothesis I intended to prove with John's experimental set up, except possibly, "How does it go, if we take seriously the business model of human happiness? How does that *go*, exactly?" The whole thing is disingenuous, because people don't just walk around *not thinking*. They betray their views on the economic model of consciousness just by espousing it in the first place. A *performative contradiction* is what they are. Feed and fuck and feed and fuck and *think about it.* FUCK.

It's possible (if I don't tire of this), that John could live in the cellar forever. But that doesn't seem plausible, given my observations of how quickly I tire of things and extrapolating from those observations to a future where I tire too of John and then kill him. It's what I pictured would happen, based on a measure of self-reflection and some god damned fucking honesty about one's thoughts that's uncommon around the contemporary academy. There would come a point, some point in the future, when I'd have to decide what to do with him. But at this particular moment, I didn't know *for certain*. There was nothing *clear and distinct* about the plan.[40] I didn't know what I wanted from him, or what his external *telos* might be. What was he doing here? We'd have to revert to the scientific definitions of causality in order to answer that question. It's funny, because the answer is obviously supposed to embody an Aristotelian final cause— what is he doing here? What is his *purpose*? *Why* did I bring him here? And I knew clearly and distinctly that the answers to these questions were ultimately Humean.

Because I don't like him.

And I think he should suffer.

Because he is usually wrong.

---

40 "Clear and distinct" is Descartes' measure of an idea's truth; if something is true or certain, the idea of it in one's mind will be clear and distinct. If an idea is clear and distinct, then it is true and possibly good. See Descartes, *Meditations on First Philosophy*, Meditation III. *Of God: That He Exists*: "The idea, I say, of this Being who is absolutely perfect and infinite, is entirely true; for although, perhaps, we can imagine that such a Being does not exist, we cannot nevertheless imagine that His idea represents nothing real to me, as I have said of the idea of cold. This idea is also very clear and distinct; since all that I conceive clearly and distinctly of the real and the true, and of what conveys some perfection, is in its entirety contained in this idea."

To give an entirely unsatisfactory answer, the causal explanation of why John is here is that I brought him here, a place where he wasn't before and now is, and he came to be here with the aid of his own legs, which were the source of his movement.[41]

The thing about proof is that there's always someone to prove it to, and I've been thinking, lately, even that isn't necessary. For if there were no one left whose opinion I wanted to shift in my favour, there would still remain a pattern of rationality whereby from one premise another is discerned. You may think there's no sense in making a purely academic point, if there's no one else to recognize it. The point can't be to demonstrate progress in my field by means of a proof to which John's suffering should contribute. However, there is a point, there is a point, there is a line, there is a tangent to my dealings with him that will be represented in the research product, regardless of whether I or John or anyone else is alive to note it.

The point of doing this, is just to do it. To have the moment exist in reality.

John has an internal *telos*. He is to be toward becoming

---

41 C.f., Socrates' expression of his disappointment with Anaxagoras from *Phaedo* 98b-d. The cause of John's sitting here with limbs bent is actually very similar: "This wonderful hope was dashed as I went on reading and saw that the man made no use of Mind, nor gave it any responsibility for the management of things. That seemed to me much like saying that Socrates' actions are all due to his mind, and then in trying to tell the causes of everything I do, to say that the reason I am sitting here is because my body consists of bones and sinews, because the bones are hard and are separated by joints, that the sinews are such as to contract and relax, that they surround the bones along with flesh and skin which hold them together, then as the bones are hanging in their sockets, the relaxation and contraction of the sinews enable me to bend my limbs, and that is the cause of my sitting here with my limbs bent."

whatever he becomes, and that's his purpose.

There's a sort of *thing* that he is, and if that's what he is, he should be it authentically.

And what he is, is the embodiment of the feed and fuck model of happiness—the economic model of success—the cave-dweller whose refusal to recognize the light outside ensures they remain captive, so long as the feed and fuck model is perpetuated.

His purpose is to be what he is.

A fat fuck who doesn't know any better than dollars.

When I opened the door to the cellar, I turned on a bright floor lamp and shone it down the stairs at him. In front of the lamp, I would present the objects he was allowed. Materialities conducive to the sustenance he'd always implied was equal to human happiness. Bread. An apple. A carton of milk. But mostly I fed John on raw potatoes. They were nutritious and tasted like dirt. It would remind him of his time on the surface of the earth, I thought.[42]

Every so often, I would wait for darkness and descend the stairs without the light. I would find John in the dark and, touching only his cock, bring him to orgasm. At first, I tried to imagine someone else I'd prefer to touch, but the habit poisoned my own libido and had to be revised. After that, it sufficed to think of myself as a farmer or large animal breeder, wanking a poorly-endowed horse to ensure the farm's survival into next season, performing a function to serve a purpose. Except in their case, the purpose was to encourage life. In my case, my function was to bring John closer to death.

A death which he conceived of as life, to be fair.

Little bits of soul on the dirt below ground.

---

42   Plato, *Phaedo*, 109c: "We, who dwell in the hollows of it, are unaware of this and we think that we live above, on the surface of the earth."

Socrates tells us in the *Phaedo* that the philosopher is practicing for death, in that the philosopher thinks abstractly and is unattached to their physical body. But there's something to that theory that people always miss. The philosopher does not, in fact, tend toward death, because by the same story, the soul is meant to separate itself from the body, in such a way as to *continue to live*. The philosopher tends toward life, by impugning the body. The body is death, and what really is life, is freedom from it. By tying John ever closer to his body, I would assure his death. There would be no separation of the soul from that body. He would become encased in his physical form, and only when he was so tied down to physicality that no hope of escape seemed possible, then I could take his physical form, assured that the soul would go with it. *Like Socrates' ghosts who wander the graveyard at night.*[43]

I told John that everything he'd done before his time in the cellar had taken place before his birth. I told him that he was remembering things he had forgotten, when he descended into life. I convinced him that this was all there was to live for—the feed and fuck model of life he could only conceive of in the abstract, during the time before. Now reborn, he lived it, and I told him if he lived it well enough, he would be happy, just as he'd always argued in his life before life, the illusion of before.

I trained him to notice the slight changes in his physical form, perceived internally without the aid of hearing, sight, touch or taste. I taught him that the sense of touch is all that pervades the physical form, and the only sense requisite to continued life.[44] I

---

43 See my previous study, earlier in this volume, "Soul Mates I Kill Shots."

44 Cf. Aristotle's *De Anima*, 413b4-9: "The primary form of sense is touch, which belongs to all animals. Just as the power of self-nutrition can be separated from touch and sensation generally, so touch can be

taught him that the artificial accumulation of wealth was meant to assure the soul's attachment to the body, so that perhaps, someday, he might learn to perceive correctly, in the same way he used to before he was born into this current state. Because of the angle of my floor lamp, John came to see in light and darkness only, and I told him that his memories of colours were from a place beyond life itself. It would require him to ascend to an enhanced bodily form, beyond the touch-based mode of perception he'd become accustomed to in the cave.

"You've been furnished with all of the senses you need to be happy, according to the economic model you've ordained. You have the sense of touch, which is sufficient for this world. If there were anything beyond, you'd have the sense to know it."

"Tell me about the colours," he'd say.

And I would quote Socrates in the *Phaedo*, reading, "Well then, my friend, in the first place it is said that the earth, looked at from above, looks like those spherical balls made up of twelve pieces of leather; it is multi-coloured, and of these colours, those used by our painters give us an indication; up there the whole earth has these colours, but much brighter and purer than these; one part is sea-green and of marvelous beauty, another is golden, another is white, whiter than chalk or snow; the earth is composed also of the other colours, more numerous and beautiful than any we have seen."[45]

"How do I get to see the world like that?" he would ask.

"Forsake the feed and fuck model of happiness," I told him.

"But I would die," he'd object.

"And you would be happier dead."

---

separated from all other forms of sense. (By the power of self-nutrition we mean that part of the soul which is common to plants and animals: all animals whatsoever are observed to have the sense of touch.)"

45 Plato, *Phaedo*, 110b-c.

He did not catch on to the perversion of Plato's theory of immortality which I'd taught him. From me, he learned the only way to see the true colours of the earth would be to trap the soul in the body, by tending to the body alone, and by ignoring the needs of the soul. I told him that every time he asked me about the colours, he was tending to the wants of the soul, and that he should be punished—physically, so that the touch sensations would negate the existence of soul outside the part of the body subject to pain. Because it was a similarity between mine and Plato's theories that, in the experience of pain, the soul becomes attached to its physicality.

"Why is it that both pleasant and unpleasant sensations trap the soul?" he'd ask me. "Wouldn't the soul want to abandon a body that's in pain?"

"This is basic psychology you need to accept. The soul is present in all extreme bodily sensations; it doesn't care whether they are positive or negative. We have determined this through experimentation."

And he believed me, because he believed in the empirical science based on the fundamental premise that materiality was *all that was* or could be counted. He remembered that premise from before his descent.

I found it did not matter so much if I kept my theories straight, because he could believe one thing at one time and its opposite at another, and never consider the contradiction between them.

When he said he didn't want his penis touched, I would tell him he was a very bad man, that the sensations were objectively pleasant,[46] that his soul would be harmed if he resisted its attachment to the body.

---

46 I was of course, being ironic, in honour of Dora. See "Ode to Dora (The Case Study of Sigmund)."

I gave him objects of touch and allowed him to assign a value to each of them. Swatches of fabric from the craft store. Plastic and metal objects of various textures. Sometimes he would offer them to me in trade, to hear more about the colours. Until one day I took them all and told him, quoting Socrates, "The very hollows of the earth, full of water and air, gleaming among the variety of other colours, present a colour of their own so that the whole is seen as a continuum of variegated colours."

Without his objects, however, he quickly became unhappy again, with merely an imagination and nothing to perceive.

"Give me my objects back," he would insist.

"You've traded them away, and your soul as well."

"My soul as well?" He was surprised.

"Yes, your soul! The textures were all that kept it near to your perceiving touch, and now that you have nothing to sense, it wanders about the cave, lonely, and wondering why you cast it out, preferring objects from your imagination instead." I laughed at him, mimicking his ability to spout falsehoods, to place blame in the most convenient place, and to appeal to emotion in order to ensure the focus of one's subject is always upon the matter at hand and never on the hand that matters.

John cried, and I told him it was good, because it was another texture he could sense. But also that he should do it silently, lest his hearing attempt to usurp the pleasure that rightfully belonged to touch.

At night, when he thought he was sleeping, I would open the door to the cellar, shine the light down the stairs, and project to him the silhouette of some familiar object. In the morning, he would tell me about the dream he'd had, about the time before— the time before his birth inside the cave.

"If you ever want to go back," I said, "I'll prepare you a special liquid which, through its power to light up your sense of touch throughout your internality, will once and for all tie your soul to your body and activate the senses you believe you once had."

"I'll be able to see the colours?" he asked.

"If your soul is sufficiently attached to your body."

"Or else the liquid won't reach my soul to medicate it." He was making his own inferences now, based upon my premises.

"That's right."

From then on, he went cheerfully about his days, eating what he was given and insisting even more that he liked it. When I went to stimulate his genitals, he would insist on doing it himself.

"That way, my hands and my penis will both feel each other, and nothing external should lure my soul away," he reasoned.

In between feeding and fucking, he'd sit quietly, for hours, focusing on sensations alone.

And when it came time for John to die, he insisted I bring him a bath.

"If my body is surrounded by liquid, the liquid we use to trap my soul won't escape into the air," he had theorized on his own. I prepared him the concoction that was given to Socrates by the guards at the end of the *Phaedo*. And in one final act of confident miscomprehension, he spoke his final words:

"Do not forget to give my cock to Asclepius; for I haven't paid off my debts."[47]

That's how it was that after several months, John, who had once been known as "The Axe" for his ruthless budget cuts to higher education, died, alone in my cellar, in a kiddie pool of

---

47   This is a bastardization of Plato's *Phaedo*, 118a, the death of Socrates: "As his belly was getting cold Socrates uncovered his head—he had covered it—and said—these were his last words—'Crito, we owe a cock to Asclepius; make this offering to him and do not forget.'"

lukewarm water, from self-induced hemlock poisoning.
Fucking cunt.

7

God is a Novel He Didn't Read and now I'm Going to Fucking Burn Him

Quick, what's the difference between burning a book and burning a man?

The screaming.

THE LAUGHTER.

Let's talk about books for a minute. Because even the analytic materialist reductionists admit that books contain thoughts, and if books contain thoughts, that makes them minds, where minds are defined as the things where thoughts are. But those boring people thereby conclude that there's some kind of connection existing between my consciousness and that which contains my surplus data, but they refuse to admit that it's anything more interesting than that I write things in my Notes to remember them. (Because I have external memories, it is therefore possible to embody mind in a mechanical device.)[48] But that's not what *it is*.

If there is a being whose essence is its existence then existence either isn't a predicate or is not an accidental predicate; it is an *essential* predicate and that means that its essence is *it is*.

---

48 See the materialist version of the extended mind theory; it's all over the god damned place.

It is much more than that.

Sit down for a minute, sir, and let me tell you, let me tell you about the order of the universe and all that it contains. Let me tell you about how man (humanity, *anthropos*) embodies the divine and enacts its own version of demiurgic activity in the creation of a wholly new life form that we're going to call *the book*.

That is, before we burn it.

It's such a pity that so many books are burned for their political content. Child's play. At the end of it all there are so many more interesting philosophical questions than what happens when groups of people get together. And that's exactly when politics happen. But the preconditions! First there must be physics and second, it must behave. The combinations come and make it chemical and biological. Consciousness is an opportunistic infection of some of the biological, a biological entity complex enough in its composition to bear the weight of it. And all you want to know is if some consciousness or other is doing it *wrong*?

There are so many feelings to be had at the lower levels first.

So many heresies to burn.

People unite around books, because that's what aligns their consciousnesses toward a common world.

Let's live in it.

Aristotle formulized the purposiveness of the natural world and identified at every level a final cause.[49] Better than the

---

49 Aristotle, *Metaphysics*, 983a24-b1: "Evidently we have to acquire knowledge of the original causes (for we say we know each thing only when we think we recognize its first cause), and causes are spoken of in four senses. In one of these we mean the substance, i.e. the essence (for the 'why' is referred finally to the formula, and the ultimate 'why' is a cause and principle); in another the matter or substratum, in a third the source of the change, and in a fourth the cause opposed to this, that for the sake of which and the good (for this is the end of all generation and change)."

preconditions, he specified what it's *all for*. Consciousness has its directionality, and so does everything else besides. Some of what consciousness is exists externally to it, without which it would be nothing. Consciousness is fundamentally consciousness *of*. And so we might think, along with Merleau-Ponty, that what's important is we are directed toward a common world.[50]

And oh, that seemed like enough for a while.

That seemed like enough.

Except it's not enough to have all the same objects, we all want to *be the same thing*. The basis of every union, the elimination of self in favor of disindividuation. I don't *want* to be a one. I want to be *a many*. I want to be God, and God is all. I want to be all and that means ridding myself of myself by *possessing the consciousness of other*s, not like an object. Not possession like an object, not at all.

Socrates' little demon was his disindividuation, his move away from one into the all.

Some rationality he tapped into.

They used to call it the *logos*.[51]

And everyone since then has called it God.

The God at the end of it all.

---

50 "In the experience of dialogue, there is constituted between the other person and myself a common ground; my thought and his are inter-woven into a single fabric, my words and those of my interlocutor are called forth by the state of the discussion, and they are inserted into a shared operation of which neither of us is the creator. We have here a dual being, where the other is for me no longer a mere bit of behaviour in my transcendental field, nor I in his; we are collaborators for each other in consummate reciprocity. Our perspectives merge into each other, and we co-exist through a common world." Maurice Merleau-Ponty, *The Phenomenology of Perception*, tr. Colin Smith (New York: Routledge, 2002), p. 413.

51 Ἐν ἀρχῇ ἦν ὁ λόγος, καὶ ὁ λόγος ἦν πρὸς τὸν θεόν, καὶ θεὸς ἦν ὁ λόγος

God at the end of a free fall.

God as the trees lack the sky.

God as the little man withers away at his toils, his wants, and he dies.

Wherever there's a direction, that's where God is.

Is there somewhere that your thoughts were going?

Mine were.

I'm going to take you with me.

We force them all along with us.

Become me, I say as I write.

Think these thoughts along with me, together, unite.

We'll become the all as well.

We'll all follow the same path.

We'll travel along in a common direction.

And at the end.

I'll be the thing you find out.

I'll be the everything we all feel we once were and could be.

Before you took on your flesh form and thence became lonely.

Consciousness is always consciousness of.

And I will be all consciousness.

What they mean when they say they have failed to be Gods.

Another subjectivity as object is just possession as if to own.

But if we take subjectivity as subject, possession as if to be.

Think with me think with me think with me.

Think about control and all the books *you can't put down*.

I'm the one who won't let you.

Think about it.

Before we burn it down.

I am the demiurge that creates life forms to infect your consciousness and move it in *my* direction. I am the ground at the end of your fall. I am the force that moves you. I am *the way in which things seem to go.*

I am the God that failed you.

If we knew what books were, we wouldn't cry on the news when they burn, we would take our vengeance on their murderers.

Of course, some books don't deserve to live.

Some people either.

They say there's no such thing as creation *not* ex nihilo. That all we do is arrange the parts.

And I'm going to fucking burn him.

You know him you know him you know him, you know this motherfucker.

He started as a faculty member, and fuck, it's never been clear to me how people get that far if they don't like what they're doing, but someday, they just turn and become people who like money and power instead of truth and off they go, into the administration, to push papers around. To squeeze all those papers together and hope money comes out. To hide most of that money in their shoes before they leave the office, only to come back the next day and see if they can't squeeze any more money out of that same stack of papers, because indeed *not all text is the same* when it's time to calculate its value.

Some combinations are better than others.

He looks too young for his age, but it's not because he's had an easy life; it's because his soul is underdeveloped.

He used to seem nice, but his eyes changed, and now you wonder if there's something new in there if anything, some kind of smaller, worse creature controlling the works from the inside, and they closed the holes a little bit, so that no one could see what he's up to in there. But you can still tell, because there's just that one section where the light gets in and out, and so you know there's something going on in there.

It's the waxy complexion that gives him away most of all, because you know what, the physiognomists were right about one thing: you can sometimes see the soul of someone through their physicality, and while he used to seem bright and responsive to touch, now he looks like if you poked him, the indent would stick in his marshmallow flesh.

But that'll just make him so much easier to burn.

He says things like, "In my meeting with John," in that tone, that tone indicating he thinks it will have impressed you to know, to know he was in a meeting, because it was with John, because he's internalized the hierarchy to such an extent that he thinks you'll find it impressive that he had a meeting with John, even though John is just some other fuck who didn't enjoy death in the cellar after all. And he thinks, and he thinks, and he thinks you'll be impressed by that instead of dismissive.

Because he turned away from it.

Because there's no good left in him, just wax.

Not just in the eyes but in the skin as well, there's something in there staring out of every pore and when you look at it, it squirts an oily substance through the hole, because it thinks that way that you can't see it, but all it does is show you that it's in there, prove to you that it's in there, or rather who's in there, trying to obscure the view.

That's where the waxiness comes from, the oily sheen.

How close to the surface of the skin are they all living?

If it is many of them.

It could just be one in the centre, with many tendrils.

A nervous system become so nervous it had to make up for itself.

And now I've got to burn him.

Here's an experiment for you: how does a whiny motherfucker burn?

How many licks of the flame does it take to get to the centre of John's little bitch boy?

And it would all be very on purpose.

Substantial, not accidental at all.

That's the thing about philosophy. We don't do anything by accident. A person doesn't accidentally learn some ancient languages, read some texts, leave the logic out overnight and come along in the morning only to find an inference has happened without them. Universal quantifiers aren't just discovered in the wild. The philosopher fucking *does it* all. It is very much a deliberate enterprise. Just like this burning.

I've set the burn points so many and so far apart. "Clearly on purpose," they'll say, as they always do when there are multiple start points. But there's a reason we do that, and it's because bitches burn better that way. Set them all aflame and see what sticks. And if there's blood left anywhere, they'll find the benzos in him. There'll be a burning bitch with benzo blood all over the damn place.

It was hard to get the pills in him, too. Ever since I lost my office, the home laboratory has had to make some adjustments for budgetary concerns. That includes drug administration policies. Yes, of course it's the subjects who'll suffer, along with my hand, because whiny bitches have sharp teeth, but when cost is a concern, you drug your whiny bitches orally. And the sounds he made! They obviously had to stop.

"Why are you doing this?"

"People are doing this all over the country."

"What do you plan to gain from this?"

"I need to reconcile the budget shortfall."

"This feels personal."

"I promise it isn't."

It is.

His worse mistake was just being one of a many.

My mistake was not burning him sooner.

What even is it to burn a man, if it's not to burn a library, some assemblage of consciousness manifested in physical form and held in readiness for the benefit of any who pay it mind?

But not this guy.

His own thoughts couldn't fill a page. The thing is, some people have so many thoughts they can afford to offload some into books and other repositories of thought. But this man ran out of thoughts years ago. He continues to spew, but what's coming out of him in such great volumes couldn't be called consciousness, what remains isn't anything at all. If anything, it's the unconscious attempting to contaminate the rest of us with its amplitude.

A song that has volume but no melody.

What's left when there's no more soul?

This guy.

He's a book with only one-dimensional characters, in which nobody does what a human would do, and in the climactic ending, the main character invests in a vacation property.

He is exactly the kind of book that should burn.

But what is the point of it all?

What are we to learn from this experiment?

Whether the right book is worth more than the wrong man?

We already know this.

He doesn't, though, and the point is to prove it.

The thing about expanding someone's consciousness is that it has to be done alongside a volition. You have to actually pick up the book and let it happen.

Maybe if I called it a "report," he'd pick it up. Maybe if a man had written it, the words would mean something to him. Maybe if, as he were reading, he could imagine a lower intonation giving voice to the phonemes, the weight of those ideas might find some uptake in his consciousness.

Or maybe just burn him.

But he's not the only one of his kind.

There are many *copies* of the same book.

And so many instances of this man.

Whatever happens to *Being and Nothingness* when you burn one copy…

Is what will happen to this guy when he burns.

Does that mean he lives on?

No, but his kind will.

And he is nothing over and above that.

There's no unity in his disintegration by fire, no coming together, no bond, no becoming more, not better.

Just less.

And *less and less and less and less and less and less and less*.

Each man a suicide for the sake of the worst.

Instead of being God, they wish to be nothing.

This is what people mean when they speak of evil.

An entity against itself, a something for a nothing, an *is* for a *not*.

There is something it's all for, but not for this guy.

A book meant to dissolve consciousness.

A slow deadening.

The blunt object resisting thought's blade.

The pot that's too small for the roots to expand in.

The lack of air underground.

He's the empty that appears when what *is* moves along.

The stagnant air of a tomb.

The oppressiveness of humidity.

The weight of your baggage.

He's the reason what could be will not.

What happens when you burn one thing of which there are many?

Not much.

"There is no record of any such catastrophe,"[52] they say of the burning at Alexandria.

The library record of his existence is the smell of burning meat.

---

52 Luciano Canfora, *The Vanished Library*, tr. Martin Ryle (Berkeley: University of California Press, 1990), p. 82.

Interim discussion: Kill the Third Man I
Suicide for the Sake of It

We cannot ignore the question, is it possible to kill *humanity*? Humans all die, by virtue of their humanity (if they were not human, they would not necessarily die, for not all non-human things do, but all human beings do die), so we might say that it's their humanity that kills them, some kind of inherent weakness they're all born with that ensures their ultimate demise.

But what of their humanity?

"You've no humanity left," one might say to a person whose acts have pushed them beyond the realm of the normal for what we call "human." But they mean to say along with Boethius that whatever you are now, it's an animal in a human body. You're beastly. And it's all right to kill you now, animal. Death penalty.

What's the death penalty for the species?

And how does one kill it?

There's the third man problem to deal with.[53]

---

53 The third man is what happens if you decide that "man" is also a man in addition to men, such that we now require a third "man" to explain relation that unites "man" and men. Aristotle, *Metaphysics*, 1038b34-1039a2: "If, then, we view the matter from these standpoints,

We know what humans have in common is their humanity. Where is that humanity? The scientists will announce it's in the body somewhere. But they're just pointing more smugly at the problem. Where in the human is its humanity and how many humans do I have to kill to rid myself of them entirely?

Kill off what makes it possible to kill them (the form of human, immortal as human is mortal).

Get out of my house, third man.

Get out of the rest of them, too.

There's nothing worse than an unwelcome species. It's invasive to the living room.

They're all in my consciousness and worse in my thoughts.

They appear most when I least want them to, and hang around past their welcome.

If there's going to be any way out of this problem, I've got to kill humanity.

You can't kill enough humans to kill humanity itself.

Or maybe you can, because if all humans are dead, their humanity will die along with them. But does it? Or is it only incidental?

Perhaps humanity retreats as the human is burning.

It hides in everyone, growing in strength and concentrating, until there's only one human left to bear all of humanity on its own.

And you burn that one too, because they're nothing more than human, just more human than the rest.

But here we might agree with the scientists, because when the humans are dead, what's to say their humanity is too?

---

it is plain that no universal attribute is a substance, and this is plain also from the fact that no common predicate indicates a 'this', but rather a 'such'. If not, many difficulties follow and especially the 'third man'."

Their bits are all over the staircase.
Their blood is all over the walls.
It smells of burnt hair in the office.
And pig roast through all of the halls.

If we as a species can't bring them back from there, perhaps it's just a matter of not having the machines to do it.

No, we must admit that I, as a human, can only kill humans, and if I want to kill humanity, I must be something better.

God.

A being toward death.

A being toward *all deaths*.

It is not just one death I'm being toward but "death," and this is again the difference between a one and a many, a particular and a universal, my own inescapable but nevertheless underwhelming death at the hand of some illness or otherwise bodily malfunction resulting in a slow shorting out. A being that is toward that small kind of death deserves to be forgotten.

I am a being toward death itself.

More than a human death, the death of humanity.

I am the God of the death of humanity.

And my creation is their destruction.

Freedom from their gaze and from their wanton acts of will.

It is not enough to have them cast their eyes down.

Burn them out and see what's left.

Is that where the human is? In the eyes?

If it were, they'd not go on living after that.

Let them wander blindly as I convert their environment to threats.

Turn the trees into knives.

Make the ground disappear.

Turn the oceans hot and then cold again.

Change the light so it breaks through their houses.

Have them run to their basements and then let them crumble.

Shake the ground until they all get mixed in.

A tomb for one and all.

Is that where the humanity is? In the corpse underground?

Take their tongues so they cannot speak, or better yet the heads.

Turn them mad.

It's funny when people say, "You're going to make me mad," when mad means not only angry but also insane, and I think they do mean to imply that, but it doesn't make any sense because the mad aren't angry; they're confused, and sad, and helpless.

And they just wish someone would let them go home.

Home to the realm of things that can't be cut and burned.

Home to the heavens above the moon where souls go when they die.

But of course it is not the souls that die. Thus it's my turn to kill that, too.

Kill the soul.

Make it a body.

Confine it to the earth.

Watch it walk around the graveyard, jealous of all the other dead.

There's nothing left for it to want to be, but nevertheless, it is unhappy.

And I will be the God of denial.

I am the master of all that is, "No."

Every negative an affront to existence.

It's non-existence now, baby.

That's what's *in*.

You're out, you mass of fleshy things you, get outta here.

And take your dead souls with you too.

Kill humanity, before it kills you.

"All humans are mortal."

Don't tell me about the *anthropos,* I was there.

And don't tell me it's just men, because it isn't.

That's what the translators want you to think.

It's humans.

I'll lurk above them in the atmosphere and knock them down as they try to ascend.

I'll bring the planets closer in, to concentrate the gravity.

I'll turn up the electric fields and split their spirits by the poles.

On one end of the earth, only positive spirits leftover.

And on the other end of the earth, only the negative.

Let them suffer being separate; opposites attract.

But in between them, a mass of resistance, reeking of the corpses they once were.

Can you imagine stepping over your own corpse to get to your loved ones?

Everything dissipates if there is nothing left to ground it.

Destroy the earth itself.

You know there's nothing in the middle except the legends that religion told us.

Time to get down there, I say.

Once my souls are concentrated in the middle, they'll all suffer.

They'll start protruding themselves in any way they can.

People will say that life is returning to the earth.

But I'll know that it's actually death.

The earth will be a war machine of treacherous terrains.

Water to kill.

Earth to kill.

Fire and air to kill.

And I'll be the one that kills them.

Back to the beginning, before the elements were separated out.

A churning mass of cosmos and the chaos that preceded the logos.

Bring it back.

It's retrofitted.

We can't just kill humanity, we must kill reason itself.

The way in which the heavens all got organized.

The linear progression from one to the other to the other.

Eliminate the harmony of their orbits.

Force only exists because I let it.

I was there before it.

I was there to let the planets form, allowed it.

And I'll undo it. Now it's done.

Now it's over.

I'm so over it.

Let chaos come again.

I will destroy humanity by destroying form itself, of which it is just one.

Just to be safe.

8

Ally's Loose Lips Sink Theseus' Ship (God Dies a Little)

Get it together, bitch! It's time to kill God.

When Nietzsche says that God is dead,[54] what he means is that we've reached the end of the tyranny of absolutes. Any and all phrases of the sort "all are" or "every one is" are over. God is truth, God is good, God is love, God is *not not not anymore*. God is dead, and I want to be God.

Of course one cannot kill humanity.

But I could kill God's women.

And don't they all look the same?[55]

Murder is a sin, but not etymologically.

The Greek word we translate as "sin" (ἀμαρτία) was an archery term, at one point, meaning to miss the mark. Someone

---

54 "But when Zarathustra was alone he spoke thus to his heart: 'Could it be possible! This old saint in his woods has not yet heard the news that *God is dead!*'" Friedrich Nietzsche, *Thus Spoke Zarathustra: A Book For All and None*, tr. Del Caro, Del Caro and Pippin eds. (Cambridge: Cambridge University Press, 2006), p. 5

55 Plato, *Timaeus*, 29d: "He was good, and one who is good can never become jealous of anything. And so, being free of jealousy, he wanted everything to become as much like himself as was possible."

noticed that we are all aiming at God and that we sometimes miss. It's our tragic flaw.

Once, when I was younger, I went to stay with a boyfriend's relatives, but we couldn't stay in the house with them, the old man said, because we were living *in sin*. Just a constant failure, when you think about it. To be fair, I missed the mark on that one, but on the other hand, that's not what he meant.[56]

I'll tell you what I have missed.

I miss being at the front of the room, where everyone thinks you know what you're talking about.

And even if they don't, they know enough not to say anything about it.

Most of the time.

(Most of the time.)

I miss teaching someone the same things I was taught, until the point where one could truly say, *we now have something in common*. Because we did. For all at once, we thought the same thoughts, and were one.

I miss propagating consciousness.

I miss being influential. I miss recognizing a good in someone that it seems everyone else has failed to appreciate, and I miss using my influence to get them something they deserve, that without me they couldn't have got.

I miss every so often revealing something to someone, something that made me human.

I miss that sometimes, we had secrets.

The borrowed respect I'd get, which wasn't granted to me as just a human but as "professor."

It's easier for a woman not to take advantage of her position,

---

56 Christians now don't care to know what their words mean, as long as they can use them to hurt someone.

because she doesn't want to fuck just anyone.

I miss looking around the room to see who's fuckable.

It's a sign of a brilliant philosopher to be fuckable.

I missed a lot of signs though, and they'll say that was my ruin.

What I don't miss, is marks.

Because as I always tried to tell them, as they started on their papers, define your terms, but don't use the dictionary. The dictionary can only tell you how words are used. It doesn't make them mean what they mean. And you can't mean to use a word with all of its definitions. So do not use the dictionary to define your terms, *tell me what you mean by them*. When they say that I'm a sinner, they meant something very different than that I missed marks.

I taught young men and women not to question their faith precisely, but *how to* do so. The distinction is clear to me. It's like teaching someone how to kill a human, should you need to do it, versus teaching them *to kill humans*, which is not at all the same curriculum; you are in the wrong department, I'm afraid.

And I am in the wrong place all together.

Except that I meant to come.

Merleau-Ponty establishes in the *Phenomenology of Perception* a habit body. Far from the usual body theories about how much body is yours, how much does your identity depend on it, etc., the point relative to me is that whatever I can habitually use to some effect seems to be and is part of my physical body.[57]

---

57 "It is precisely when my customary world arouses in me habitual intentions that I can no longer, if I have lost a limb, be effectively drawn into it, and the utilizable objects, precisely in so far as they present themselves as utilizable, appeal to a hand which I no longer have. Thus are delimited, in the totality of my body, regions of silence." Merleau-Ponty, Ibid., 95. Note, however, that Sartre mocks Merleau-Ponty's concept of the body with regard to his concept of

A numb or useless leg is not mine, whereas a tool which I have learned to use has become a part of me. If Heraclitus is right in that you cannot step in the same river twice, why do I have to be the same as myself from moment to moment? After all, "We step into and we do not step into the same rivers. We are and we are not."[58] Like the ship of Theseus, when every board is replaced on the trip to Delos and back, returning again the same but not quite.

The question, when you put these two concepts together, is *how well do I have to habituate myself to externalities of a certain sort, to alter my physical form*?

Make it all together inhuman.

Make it demonic.

I started by pulling my hair back and painting my whole head. It would never do if I weren't used to the feeling of it. But my hair was too uncomfortable and took too much washing, so I got rid of that. I understand why people shave their heads before suicide; it's like a half death already. *Only so much more to go.* I'd become unrecognizable to myself.

"double sensations". A "double sensation" occurs when one has the simultaneous sensations of touching and being touched. Sartre notes that such phenomena disappear if, before one touches one's own leg, one administers morphine or is just cold: "Of course when I touch my leg with my finger, I realize that my leg is touched. But this phenomenon of double sensation is not essential: cold, a shot of morphine, can make it disappear. This shows that we are dealing with two essentially different orders of reality. To touch and to be touched, to feel that one is touching and to feel that one is touched—these are two species of phenomena which it is useless to try to reunite by the term 'double sensation'. In fact they are radically distinct, and they exist on two incommunicable levels." Jean-Paul Sartre, *Being and Nothingness*, tr. Hazel Barnes (New York: Washington Square Press, 1993), p. 402.

58 Heraclitus fragments in Patricia Curd, *A Pre-Socratics Reader*, 2nd ed. (Indianapolis: Hackett, 2011), p. 45.

I'd become the demon loose in the nunnery.

Red all over with Rugers for hands.

I walked around the apartment like that for days, becoming something other, something inhuman that preys on them. As it's really unfortunate that humanity has no natural predator. In order to become humanity's predator, it's imperative to integrate the divine into one's fleshly form, but this damn apartment and its familiar things kept dragging me back into mundanity. There are two possible ends to becoming feral, animal or God. *I would be the latter.*

Outside, amongst the other creatures, I killed what I could with my new hands of violence. The religious as well as the biologists tell you to look at the particular parts of a human body and determine their purpose, but as I was becoming so adept with my pistols, we have to look there instead. Their weight had already strengthened my arms, so it felt like nothing to lift them, and if I set them down, it was like something was missing—an arm too light, suddenly missing a hand. I no longer had to think about my aim; whatever I thought to kill, so it died. The movement, fluid and automatic, did not rest on some interior rational calculation, became as natural as putting one foot in front of the other.

And so I knew that I had changed.

I threw off my clothes and painted myself the colour of the demons, as they were represented in art. (It is not, in fact, likely that the demons are coloured at all, not bound as we are to this limited physicality.) But part of our identities are socially constructed, and while the theorists often remark on this as being some kind of passive process we have to accept (our identity depends in part on what people might think of us), it is rather an active process through which I decide how other humans will conceive of me by triggering their habitual concepts and associations.

Because other people believe that the demons are red, so too would I be.

It's important to feel understood.

I pictured myself, in the nunnery, like a weasel that sneaks into the farmer's barn and snuffs all the chickens, one by one, too stupid to run. But the difference, of course, is my choice of prey. Anyone can kill a chicken; it takes something more to kill a gross number of humanity's representatives to the divine.

Hypocrites, liars, deluded and meek individuals, sent to sequester themselves away from the strong, thinking that there, away from the humans, they'll escape evil and themselves, becoming something other, all wearing the outer flesh form of someone better, claiming power over others by reason of their weakness, lording subordination over domination, and propagating the ideal to all who will listen, that, "You too can defile yourself to this extent."

But no.

I knew it was time to go when my stigmata began.

When men experience the stigmata, a centrifugal force applies which forces the blood to the extremities—hands, feet, and head. But when women experience the same phenomenon, the negative force applies. Blood from the extremities pools in our centres and runs down our legs from the middle.

I mixed the blood with my paint and ensured it was evenly spread.

The scent will mark my arrival to the bloodless.

Just as the Virgin Mary cries tears of blood, so too will my blood have to be cleansed from the church floor.

Hairless, red and ready, I slid silently through a basement window. Finding the stairs, I ascended. I ascended again.

Up and up and up and up I went.

Until I found a room with a woman in it.

And made it so there wasn't.

I reached into my Godhead, that divine triangle, and used the holy water from it to anoint her forehead with the cross.

So that their God would know which ones were mine.

It didn't matter if all of them ran at the sound, though not all of them did. There would be enough of them to say the place was full of death.

And I, full of life and the lives and the souls of many.

I took more of them.

In the second room, I wrote SIN on the wall.

A little joke, because I did not miss.

A good many of them prayed and kissed their rosaries.

As if the way to please a God was to take him in your mouth.

(They mistook their God for man.)

It quickly became obvious that I wasn't the only source of blood here.

Floods of it came from every door I passed.

And in this one, big eyes looked back at me.

"Hello," she said.

"Hello."

She still wore the full habit, as if she hadn't prepared for bed along with the others. Or as if she'd put it back on, just for me.

"Stay with me a minute," she said, trying to delay me.

But time isn't anything anymore.

And I wanted to get to know her better.

Her name was Ally, and she said she thought she knew me, from her prayers.

"I've seen you dancing, just beyond what I can control," she said and stared.

Her mouth tasted like blood, and so did her pussy.

She asked me, at one point, "Why?"

And I told her, "Because you're the one who made them hate me."

I meant it of every person there.

But the look in her eyes reminded me that everyone is a one, that no matter how many times they all had done me wrong, she had not yet. That for every person alive there's one more, one more that hasn't hurt you. As long as we're alive, there still exists some future time in which someone could decide not to wrong you.

"You don't have to believe that," Ally said, and I knew for fuck's sake that she meant it. Ally said it, and I believed her. I believed them every time. *Do you know how much effort it takes, not to be deceived?*

Oh God, Ally, why couldn't you be one of a many?

I knew what she'd meant to say: *It doesn't have to be this way.* And I knew from the look on her face that she had within her mind a vast set of possible futures, a number of ways in which things could occur. An infinite set of things that could happen.

But she also knew she couldn't say that exactly, because I'd know. That she knew she was wrong about that.

On the contrary, there were a finite number of words she could speak, and she knew I'd take those ones badly. She knew that of all the words to say, those would come off as *cliché,* and for good reason, because of all the times they'd been said before. She knew if she said them, I'd be reminded of all the times someone in her same position had spoken the exact same words to someone just like me, and she knew that meant the end. She saw the end coming, and she thought she could avoid it with synonyms.

But today is the day that universals die.

Binding them to finitude, for the long run, for all the wrong reasons.

The fact of the matter is, Ally, that there's no way out of it. And if you didn't know that too, you wouldn't have said it that way. If the future were that uncertain, you'd never know there was something to fear in it.

Oh, Ally, I wish I could tell you everything.

We have to accept that this is where we both are, and neither of us can get out of it. I thought of the past, when I first left for university. Epictetus said they would mock me, and so they did. But it didn't matter.[59]

What are you going to do with that? Father asked of my degrees, because he didn't conceive of the infinite possibilities Ally did.

Ally doesn't know there aren't actually any alternative futures.

But I left all the same, and I made this life happen. I made all of it happen. I *forced it*. Because there have got to be possibilities. That than which nothing greater can exist is better if it exists in

---

59 Epictetus, *Enchiridion*: "Do you think that you can act as you do and be a philosopher, that you can eat, drink, be angry, be discontented, as you are now? You must watch, you must labor, you must get the better of certain appetites, must quit your acquaintances, be despised by your servant, be laughed at by those you meet; come off worse than others in everything—in offices, in honors, before tribunals. When you have fully considered all these things, approach, if you please—that is, if, by parting with them, you have a mind to purchase serenity, freedom, and tranquility. If not, do not come hither; do not, like children, be now a philosopher, then a publican, then an orator, and then one of Caesar's officers. These things are not consistent. You must be one man, either good or bad. You must cultivate either your own reason or else externals; apply yourself either to things within or without you—that is, be either a philosopher or one of the mob."

reality and therefore that than which nothing greater exists does exist,[60] and so does a better future for me.

And when I couldn't afford new books, father told me, *Perhaps now you'll recognize what kind of person you are*. And by that he meant, where I'd come from.

But there aren't any actual barriers, are there? I assured myself. There's nothing physically in the way of my doing this; nothing to stop me; no impediments, no hindrances that can't be overcome, there's nothing that my will can't supersede.

You knew what you were getting into, the woman in finance told me when I brought her my calculations, about how the scholarships, the bursaries, and the loans all together still didn't cover the bills she'd sent me. When I explained to her that little bits of paper couldn't possibly undo all I'd done so far—or could they? I came to her as a person, and she treated me like *something else. Was that the moment that led to this one?*

There is no other sort of thing to be, Ally. Not for me and not for anyone. Don't you recognize all of the circumstances that had to align for us to come together? The great convergence of all that was to a singular point in time where everything had to happen. Everything was headed in this direction. There was only ever one possible future, and here we are, negating it.

I am.[61]

Ally, I only wish there were someone else to be, something else to be done. But there are forces, constant forces, keeping us in position. Ally thought if she appealed to the existentialist in me, I'd recognize that radical freedom, as the gallows comes into view, when as long as I've got volition left, I can will my body to reject the fates.

---

60 Anselm!

61 I.e., it is.

But Ally, if you run away from the hangman, they'll just shoot you.

She thought, all this time, no one was seeing the human in me, and that if she were the first one, I'd see hers too.

That's the problem, Ally. I already do.

It is true that when they treat you like something else, you become that. A number, a metric, a profit margin. For a time, I was the best number I could be. I had the best metrics, and I produced. May all that I have done since then prove again that my research is relevant, impactful, *strategic*, even.

Radical freedom is when *they* decide it still doesn't matter.

Radical freedom is when *you* recognize that no matter the cause and effect relations you attempt to enact in the universe, the whims of another can quash them.

Radical freedom is the freedom *of others* to declare the null hypothesis, a death that fails to live up to anticipation, an ending where it shouldn't be.

I never would have forced my own way to the margins. I didn't choose to kill everything within the bounds from which I'd been ousted. I was put there, as we all were, with a recognition of infinity confined by limitations.

I'm so tired of the confines, Ally.

I'm so tired of becoming what I've been told, or something else in reaction to it.

You don't have to believe that, she said. But what she meant was, *you could choose to be wrong.*

Never.

Never fucking ever, Ally.

If God is truth, maybe I do believe. I knew that as Ally held me, I'd forget soon enough why I'd come here. And I knew well enough what would happen if I were still alive in the morning.

Because we can predict the future. It's just more of the past. I felt myself becoming visible as the paint rubbed off my skin and on to hers, her hair, her bed, her clothes. I knew it should make me feel more human, but the more of my tears I let run, the more humanity I lost in the mixture.

Or so I chose to conceive it.

As Ally had chosen to confine herself here.

Death was freedom for both of us, and I think she understood. She let me take my gun back, and she let me put it under her habited body.

I put the barrel of my Ruger in her as she came.

My bullet forged a path from one set of Ally's lips to the other, my divine light to shine through.

The blood at each end of it tasted the same.

And in the morning, when the other nuns came, they'd see that Ally had done her part to make me see the sin of it all.

But I am animal become God.

The condemnation of humanity.

Not God, but the red weasel loose in his house.

9

Appendix A

Editor's Note: The following typed pages were found among the professor's effects. The reader should be aware that most scholars consider them spurious. Worse than esoteric, these bits and pieces only indirectly refer to the events leading up to the professor's demise. There has been no definitive conclusion to the matter of when the professor might have written them. And while the professor wasn't known as a garrulous smatterer, the awkwardness of these revelations don't reflect the professor's usual obscurity. Rather, appearing out of context and with no account for their chronology, we caution the reader against taking any biographical details that follow as authoritative, gathered as they are from text that is almost certainly corrupt, if not fraudulent (likely the work of a junior scholar attempting to emulate the professor, with the aim of causing strife in the institution).

I must write the things I presently write, for I know that despite all appearances, my consciousness is not universal territory. I recognize that for all the shouting I've done, there may yet be some individuals who are completely unaware of my struggles with the institution, their implications for the discipline as a whole, and the consequences I've suffered personally.

Why did you do it? They'll ask of my experiments. They'll act as if I should give them a rational response. *There was something I wanted to accomplish. I imagined that by doing the things I did, that I would accomplish said things. And then I set upon doing them.*

But the question is wrong, isn't it?

And so is that all-too-typical response.

In actuality, there's nothing that I wanted to accomplish, and there was no way to do it. There's no such calculus of human behaviour, and it's obvious when you think about it.

When someone commits acts of atrocities, it's never for a *reason*. What we call "reasons" in those cases aren't reasons at all, but irrationalities. When someone commits a criminal act, we ask ourselves what motivates them, and there's never a rational explanation. The rational murderer defies our conception. Dostoevsky's Raskolnikov is a mythical figure for a *reason*.[62]

No, the way that criminals are motivated, the reasons we give for their actions are always also vices. The criminal acts for greed; the criminal acts for vengeance; the criminal acts for lust. We call them reasons, but they're not. They're tendencies developed over time and which survive through habit, and which we claim as explanations when all we've done is restate the

---

62   The reference is to *Crime and Punishment*. [Editor's note: The reference is too obvious, and the author too quick to point out its source. This footnote is evidence that the entire text is the work of a smug student.]

actions themselves, but now calling them by the universal term for individual actions—a character trait. And what we all should notice but haven't yet, is that human motivations don't change just because something is a crime or isn't. When someone isn't breaking the rules, we say that they acted with reasons. There was something they wanted to accomplish and some way in which they intended to accomplish it, then they set upon it. But when the act is all of a sudden criminal, the motivation becomes animal, emotional, irrational and wrong.

I alone acted for the sake of reason. But not because of reason. For the *purpose* of reason.

There's nothing that someone wants *out* of revenge, a reason *for* the revenge. Revenge is what occurs *despite* reason, and *now so am I.*

When I was young, very young, and I didn't understand the world and its people and their reasons, they—those very same people—told me it'd get better. I'd have to go to university, where everyone was smarter and therefore less cruel to each other. And when I got there, I thought it was true. I went through all those degrees, each one smarter than the last, each one set against a backdrop of human intelligence—rationality—that hit its maximum at the university. But to be the student was not yet to attain that apex. At the university itself, there's so much further to climb.

Students occupy the bottom rung of rationality.

Oh, but when they show promise.

How hard it is not to love them.

Irrational as it may be.

It made sense to think that the university was the most rational place in the world, and that's what I said when they hired me. "This isn't a rational place," they said, and I thought they meant the state.[63] "But I'll be at the university," I said, as if that protected me from the irrationality without. And it made sense to think the higher up in the university you went, the more rationality you'd find.

But I was wrong.

It isn't the case that men change their motivations depending on whether they're committing criminal acts or not. It isn't the case that the formula applies—motive, means, action—not even a little, not even at all.

I was teaching people to believe that, despite all that they'd held, rationality would win out. It was the thing humanity had on everyone else, and the most rational of the humans would be happiest of all.   At the same time, I came to notice that rationality dissipated the further up the university's hierarchy you went.

Until at the very top was a very small man who shouted downwards that all, from now on, should be in the service of irrationality.

And rationality listened.

They would say things like *budget* and *regional needs* and *second tier institution* and *cuts are coming*.

But you can't have a university without a philosophy department.

Can you?

I was crushed when they shut us down. We were the bedrock of human rationality, the locus of logic and critical thinking, the keepers of the history of thought, and the only discipline to study existence in itself, alongside knowledge itself, the true, the good, and the beautiful. It hits hard, when someone takes a cursory

---

63 [Editor's note: the professor was notoriously from out of state. This is a reference to geography and not, as some have argued, a truncated expression for "state-of-affairs."]

look at the thing to which you've dedicated your life, the thing which you have determined to be the only pursuit worth pursuing, the one thing whose *aim* is to explain why or *if* life is worth living, and decides against it. Decides it isn't worth the money. Decides it isn't worth your doing. It hits hard.

If only they could see.

I thought it was an insight I must coax them toward. With strong argumentation, clear communication, and the underlying shared premise that knowledge for its own sake is *the highest good for humanity to achieve*, I went armed against them. I wrote reports and documents, I presented any and all reasons, and the reasons weren't just any reasons but reasons which embodied the *objective good* to which all humanity aimed. But they weren't the arguments they wanted.

They wanted practical arguments, arguments aimed at maximizing utility, productivity, financial gain and demonstrable metrics of success. So I gave those to them too. I showed them how we profited—financially—and how our students met and exceeded their expectations for what they (wrongly) considered to be success, which was not at all a fulfillment of the most honorable [*sic*] human capacities, but instead to be measured by mere financial gain. I made these arguments, the ones they wanted, even though I thought they shouldn't want them.

They wanted all the wrong things and none of the right ones.

Imagine not wanting to be right.

I made the arguments in the classrooms, and I made them in the faculty senate. I made them to the men in power, and I made them to the press. I made arguments that no rational person could deny, with which no one could argue, and nevertheless...

Nevertheless, they shut us down, and me besides.

If philosophy is in my blood, the bloodline ends with me.

How could they take the most abstract of the disciplines, the one which applied to all human beings, the living and the dead, the happy and the unhappy, the rational and irrational, and call it the least useful of all? Could they not see that the fact that it was abstract meant not that it applied to no one, but that it applied to everyone? My experiments, at last, would show how universal the claims of philosophy are—*never* abstract, *always* applied, and applied to *everyone*.

But these were not their concerns. Their concerns were small and had more to do with greed, revenge and lust than they had to do with rationality. Shutting us down was their announcement that reason no longer reigns.

And there is no rational argument against reason.

For obvious reasons.

I remembered that Hume said about reason and emotion: "… reason is, and ought only to be the slave of the passions."[64]

Emotion, indeed, is the nemesis of reason; but its other nemesis is faith.

And my nemeses had both emotions and faith.

What a perfect opportunity to test Hume's hypothesis.

To think the unreasonable, one must assume the worst of men. But when I say "assume," I mean something closer to "hypothesize," for where reason failed, a new investigation was

---

64 David Hume, *A Treatise of Human Nature*, Book II, "Of the Passions": "Nothing can oppose or retard the impulse of passion, but a contrary impulse; and if this contrary impulse ever arises from reason, that latter faculty must have an original influence on the will, and must be able to cause, as well as hinder any act of volition. But if reason has no original influence, 'tis impossible it can withstand any principle, which has such an efficacy, or ever keep the mind in suspence a moment. Thus it appears, that the principle, which opposes our passion, cannot be the same with reason, and is only call'd so in an improper sense."

required.

There's a new way to answer why, and it's going to give us the new causality.

I investigated. What were the initial conditions that set in motion the series of actions that led to them killing us off, like a minor character in a novel with an anticlimactic end? What were the *feelings* that motivated those actions? What *reasons* were propped up in place of them, to serve as explanations after the fact?

First, there was fear. Our department was eliminated, because a woman told a man to cut *something*, so he did. I was eliminated, because one small man, who was afraid of another small man, told the first small man to cut *someone*, and he did. It's amazing the extent by which the powerful are motivated by fear—fear of the more powerful, whose defining quality is that they are also afraid.

When men are so afraid of each other, someone will get hurt, and in this case, it was me.

And when we ask why, we have to also ask why not. Why did I have to go, demands that we ask the question, why did someone else not? And again, we have to eliminate motive, means, and action from our causal explanation. For a while, I presented no reasons, just speculations, and for the purpose of eliciting a passion and perhaps specifically fear. *Give me something to argue against* and I'll do it. It's what I live for.

But all of it was unsatisfactory. There was no reason adequate enough to explain the damage they had done, and the motives that I found weren't anything at all. And then there was kinship. Other departments weren't eliminated, because someone had stepped in and spoken passionately in a confident tone of voice. Other people weren't eliminated, because they were either too important or too unimportant. It turned out that when the one small man told the afraid man to axe me, the afraid man was too afraid to tell him that there were so many others who should have gone first, because he was the one who had saved them *until now*.

And so, amongst everyone, I was the virtuous mean of professors, not too young, not too old, not too established, not too new, not too connected, not too disconnected, but just right.

The choice cuts of meat get butchered.

What did the afraid man have against me?

And why in the world's bastion of rationality was that becoming the question?

Resentment, quite possibly. I gathered my data.

How many arguments must an argument maker make if an argument maker is to make enough arguments to establish the value of arguments?

It wasn't about the arguments. You see, ultimately, it all came down to the fact that the afraid man had a type of woman, and I wasn't it. And I knew, because his woman had told me. He told her, and she told me. There was no report or statement to which to refer. The afraid man preferred women who were more afraid, and so I met another nemesis of reason—taste. All the women whom he preferred were preferred not in the abstract but practically as well, with positions and payments and offices, and here I was with none. He didn't like me. He resented my assertions—that I had assertions at all, and that I would assert them.

But assertions are just statements that could be true.[65]

---

65 Or written, but the point is that those fuckers thought that I should stay at home and pray. Aristotle, *De Interpretatione*, 17a1-7: "Every sentence is significant (not as a tool but, as we said, by convention), but not every sentence is a statement-making sentence (λόγος

Ultimately, it proved too difficult to argue against someone who doesn't argue against, but merely doesn't prefer you.

It is even harder to stomach I should have to contend with that, with the idea that the bloodline of rationality ends here, because I was not more afraid, a little more unreasonable.

Within the bastion of rationality, no less.

Hume's hypothesis was, in this case, right.

Because it turns out that the bastion of rationality is as irrational as the rest of it.

And there's no reason that legitimates rationality, when rationality itself is under fire.

And so I don't give up on reason. But I recognize its nemeses— faith, emotion, and taste. And I will destroy them.

Tiny seedlings of rationality emerging from the raging unreason.

I sense their warmth in particular.

And knowing I can't argue rationality back into existence, the only thing left to do is to make them feel it.

Make them feel how universal are our doctrines.

Make them feel all the matters of life and death that feed our thinking.

Let the ashes of human flourishing burn them, as I force their feet to cross them.

Make them feel not what it says, but what it *means*.

It means they're dying.

It means they're dead.

And I am all that's living.

άποφαντικός), but only those in which there is truth or falsity. There is not truth or falsity in all sentences: a prayer is a sentence but is neither true or false. The present investigation deals with the statement-making sentence; the others we can dismiss, since consideration of them belongs rather to the study of rhetoric or poetry."

They thought that if they cut me off, I'd be the one that dies.
Like the vestigial organ of an animal evolved not to need it.
This isn't to say it turns out I was keeping them alive.
They could live just fine without me, were I gone.
It is to say that without me, they'd be fine.
Unless of course, I killed them.
There's no reason why I shouldn't.

Charlene Elsby

Charlene Elsby is a Canadian data analyst and former philosophy professor. Her previous books include *Hexis, Psychros, Musos, Bedlam*, and *The Devil Thinks I'm Pretty*.

also by

Clash Books

HEXIS
Charlene Elsby

DARRYL
Jackie Ess

GAG REFLEX
Elle Nash

GENDER/FUCKING
Florence Ashley

BAD FOUNDATIONS
Brian Allen Carr

WHAT ARE YOU
Lindsay Lerman

KILL THE RICH
Jack Allison & Kate Shapiro

HIGH SCHOOL ROMANCE
Marston Hefner

PROXIMITY
Sam Heaps

BURN FORTUNE
Brandi Homan

SILVERFISH
Rone Shavers

WE PUT THE LIT IN LITERARY
clashbooks.com

@clashbooks @clashbooks /clashbooks

Email
clashmediabooks@gmail.com